A Stitch in Key Lime

Baker's Rise Mysteries

Book Ten

R. A. Hutchins

Cover Design by Molly Burton at cozycoverdesigns.com

ISBN: 9798863757643

For close knit communities everywhere,
keep looking out for each other xx

Reggie has also asked the author to thank his
adoring fans and to say that gifts of fruits and
seeds are always welcomed!
(Flora has told him to stop being so silly!)

CONTENTS

If you follow this list in order, you will have made a perfect
Key Lime Pie *to enjoy whilst you read!*

ONE

Flora didn't like to say, 'I told you so.' But it had been a very long morning and her patience was down to its last thread – ironic since the topic of the morning's heated discussion had been the imminent arrival of the 'Yarn Wars' production crew. She could have predicted the in-fighting and one-upmanship that would occur with such an infamous television crafting programme visiting the village, and that had been before Flora had been told by an extremely red-faced, fuming Betty about the extremely limited contestant places available.

"I'm sure we're all very grateful to Betty for organising the event and for liaising with the television team. I appreciate the tensions are running high and you're all keen to have a spot on the show, however, as Betty has explained, Yarn Wars are bringing two of their own contestants. Therefore only two of you lovely ladies will get a spot on the show."

'Tensions running high' must have been the understatement of the year as Hilda May hadn't stopped tapping her crochet hook on the table since she'd arrived over two hours ago, Betty hadn't even managed to finish her first scone, so great was her consternation at not automatically being a shoo-in for a spot, and Jean had been unusually abrupt. Reggie too had picked up on the atmosphere in the room and had flown from shoulder to shoulder calling each woman an "old trout" before settling his attentions on the annoying crochet hook. The feisty parrot had then proceeded to focus his efforts on dive bombing that source of metallic malaise until Flora had eventually shut him in the book nook with Adam, silently wishing she could join them both.

"Aye well, obviously since I'm organising it all I should have a spot on the show," Betty said, her grey curls bobbing voraciously, "I'm the one who's been going back and forth with them having to deal with their ridiculous demands like holding the initial rehearsals in the pub of all places."

"I do agree, the church hall would be much more

suitable," Jean piped up, "I don't know why you said yes to the Bun in the Oven in the first place."

"Well we circumcised, didn't we," Betty said impatiently.

"I think you mean compromised, Betty," Tanya said from behind the counter where she was taking a ginger sponge loaf out of the oven. She shared a wry smile with Flora as Betty continued as if the interruption had not occurred.

"Yes, exactly, that's what I said. Anyway, obviously we had to agree because they're coming in two days," Betty hurried on, "so we'll have the first day of introductions and rehearsals in the pub like the director's requested and then we'll move to the village green weather permitting or to the church hall for the actual filming."

"Well I don't think you should automatically get a spot just because you've played secretary to the whole thing," Hilda May spoke with more ferocity than usual, finally laying the abused crochet hook down on the table to pick up her now stone cold cup of tea.

"I agree," Jean said, "I'm sure we all have our own very valid reasons for needing to be in the competition line up."

Flora wondered at the force in Jean's voice and her emphasis on the word 'needing,' but had no chance to delve into this any deeper as Betty was on the defensive again.

"Luckily it's not up to you to decide," Betty replied snappily.

"Now now ladies, I'm sure the selection process will be fair and they'll judge everyone on their own merit," Flora finally interjected, though that was pure speculation on her part – she had no idea how these things really worked.

"Aye at least Rosa can't compete what with her doctor putting her on bed rest for the last six weeks of her pregnancy," Betty seemed rather too gleeful about that fact, hastily adding "bless her, I'll have to take around some of my home bakes to celebrate being crowned the Yarn Wars champion."

"Anyway," Flora said with a deliberate sense of finality as she saw Jean and Hilda gearing up for another showdown, "we've established that Sunday is the day they'll arrive, that Shona will provide the refreshments in the pub keeping the whole place solely for our use until tea time, that everything will be explained to us then. Goodness me that seems a very short list to have taken such a long time to clarify," Flora checked her watch, conscious that Naomi would be coming out of school now and heading to catch the bus home from Alnwick. They were only two weeks into the new school year and Flora's foster daughter had retreated into her shell more and more since the first day back. Adam had reassured his wife that it was just the transition into a stricter routine after a summer lazing around The Rise. They had taken a family trip, just the three of them, plus Reggie of course, down to London to see the sights but other than that the teenager had enjoyed pottering around the village learning to bake with Betty and Hilda, and to crochet with Rosa, brushing off Flora's suggestions that she might want to meet up with her friends in the bigger town. Flora had offered to drive her, to pay for cinema tickets or bubble tea, but each time had been met with vague, noncommittal shrugs or grunts. Eventually Flora had followed Adam's advice and had let the girl be – goodness knew she had already had enough upheaval in her young life and deserved a summer of peace and stability.

The afternoon's discussion had dragged on more than long enough and Flora still needed to finalise the arrangements for Sally's remission party. An afternoon tea which was to be held up at the manor house the following weekend after the madness of Yarn Wars had left the village, and when Baker's Rise would hopefully have returned to its usual sleepy, serene state. She and Tanya needed to discuss who was doing what, and to then call Sally to check on anticipated numbers so that Flora could let Genie know how many guests to expect up at the big house.

As the ladies scraped their chairs back, unsettled that it had still not been decided which of them would compete on the show and reluctant to let the actual production director make the decision, Flora thought longingly of the end of the day. In less than an hour now, Naomi would arrive at the Tearoom on the Rise, when she and Adam would help Flora to tidy and lock up the place and they could all go home for a cosy evening. At that thought Flora's mind still always jumped to her snug little sitting room at the coach house, her favourite arm chair beside the log burner and her tiny kitchen. Of course, in reality they had been living up at The Rise for months now and the newly married Reverend and Mrs. Cartwright had taken up lodging at Flora's previous dwelling. Not that Flora minded. After all, she had offered the cottage to the pair and Genie did still do an excellent job as housekeeper up at the big house. Adam had caught on quickly to his wife's nostalgia for her cosy home, though, and so had converted one of the many spare bedrooms on the first floor of the manor house into a snug family room for the three of them, complete with two sofas, Flora's old arm chair, Reggie's favourite perch and a big, wall mounted television – which admittedly had been Adam's own contribution to the room.

Nevertheless, it seemed to have done the trick and generally Flora's feelings of melancholy and homesickness for her small coach house had abated. It was only about once a week now that she inadvertently took the wrong path when she left the tearoom, turning out of habit towards her former abode rather than her new home.

"I'd like to be a fly on the wall when they choose the two who will compete in Yarn Wars," Tanya said as she wiped down the counters while Flora carried the used cups and saucers to the dishwasher, "I can only imagine the handbag fight that'll happen if Betty doesn't get her way and goodness knows how she'll take it if one of the other Women's Institute ladies decides to throw her knitting needles into the ring on the day."

"It doesn't even bear thinking about, and we haven't even heard from Lily about whether she's hoping for a spot," Flora said shaking her head, "as head of the parish council I feel obliged to be there, for the first few hours of introductions and rehearsals at least. After that I'm leaving them to it, I have no desire to give up the best part of my week refereeing a group of creaking crafters. I had my fifteen minutes of fame a while back, as you know, when I'd just arrived in Baker's Rise and had to give a rather impromptu, early morning interview for the local news station. Never again," Flora shuddered at the memory and put it back in the metaphorical box in her head where any past unpleasantness and embarrassments resided.

"Oh! I remember that," Tanya chuckled, "you were like a deer out of water."

"It's a fish out of water or a deer caught in the headlights," Flora snapped back before quickly becoming aware of her harshness and rubbing her friend's arm to soften the correction. The last thing she wanted was for she and Tanya to fall out in the way she fully expected the more mature ladies of the village to do in the coming week. Besides, it was she herself who had mentioned the incident.

No, Flora was determined to stay out of the spotlight, hoping simply that the arrival of the show's entourage would see a boost in sales in the tearoom. The rest she would let her elderly neighbours fight out amongst themselves. *Take up knitting, it's so relaxing and therapeutic…* If Flora had a pound for every time she'd been told that! Well, judging by the newfound animosity around the table today, the only therapy involved would be after the recording of the TV programme!

TWO

At least the safeguarding rules for foster carers and their families meant that there had never been any question of the whole TV crew staying up at The Rise. Flora wished the B&B in Witherham the best of luck dealing with all of their demands, as she heard the show's director, Bob Grimes asking Shona for his second scotch on the rocks of the day – and it was only ten in the morning! Shona politely declined, though the smile with which she graced the demanding man never reached her eyes, presumably since he had helped himself to the first glass when she was busy carrying bacon rolls through from the kitchen upon their arrival.

Grimes was a man of girthy proportions, not matched

by his height – that is to say, he was almost as wide as he was tall. As if to compensate for his limited stature, he projected his voice as if he were performing opera to a crowd of hundreds. Indeed, whether the man was demanding a refill of the hard stuff or introducing his team, he had the volume of an auspicious orator. The net result of this, of course, was to set one of Flora's headaches off within the first half an hour of being stuck in the pub with him, the only silver lining being that she hadn't brought Reggie, who would've been sure to take vociferous offense to the man's assertive tone.

Grumbling loudly about the distinct lack of refreshments on offer – there were plenty, teas, coffees, juices, but he was referring to the old Scottish 'water of life' that Shona, now standing with hands on hips, resolutely refused to furnish him with – Grimes launched into an introduction of the production team. As he spoke, the man began sweating profusely, the heavy droplets dripping conspicuously into his moss green cravat, as if the exertion of remembering his colleague's names and roles was simply too much.

"So, here we have er… um… Chris, he's new to the role of runner."

"Runner?" Betty interrupted, clearly bored now that

the cheese scones had run out and keen to get to the business of choosing contestants, "What's that? Marathons and the like? Aren't you too old to be a runner?"

The man in question, a tall, lanky, forty-something, around Flora's age in fact, sent a scowl towards the group of old ladies, causing Hilda May to pipe up, ""No, Agnes Cauldfield's brother took it up at seventy! Has a medal and everything."

Grimes looked perplexed, Chris looked incensed, and Flora felt the need to explain, "No, a show runner is like a general assistant, they run errands, look after the cast and crew, basically make sure things run smoothly."

"Oh, a dogsbody!" Betty nodded as if that clarified everything, completely oblivious to the dark look that the man in question shot her.

"Um, yes well," Grimes seemed to have completely lost his train of thought now, mopping his leaking brow with a mottled handkerchief. He flew through the names of the other team members, Kirsty his assistant, Angus on camera and so on, until he was interrupted by the door to the pub being thrown open. There was a long moment before anyone appeared, as if the person in question wanted to make a grand entrance, before a man well into his seventies appeared, beaming at them all through a forced smile which threatened to crack his caked-on, orange foundation, layered as it was over fake tan of an even deeper hue.

Hushed shock filled the room, not least because the man was sporting a turquoise lamé suit and what was clearly a very blonde toupée, set on his head at an unfortunately jaunty angle. Indeed, the only sound in that moment was Jean's sharp intake of breath, which caused Flora to drag her attention from the newcomer and onto her friend. The shopkeeper was blushing from neck to temple, something Flora had never seen the usually staid Scotswoman do, her eyes glazed in seemingly starstruck adoration. Flora couldn't help her own wide-eyed expression, but no one else seemed to have noticed Jean's reaction, being as they were all focused on the man in the doorway.

Standing completely still for a moment as if to allow all assembled to drink in his image, the newcomer then introduced himself with a flourish and a bow as "Bruce Evangelista, host with the most."

Grimes appeared to groan ominously, his whole body vibrating with the emotion and his previously booming voice suddenly croaky, "I'm going to need that whisky now… and hurry up about it!"

"And I'll have whatever fine chardonnay you have chilled, my good woman," Evangelista ignored the director's comment and aimed his request at Shona.

The landlady bit down whatever remark was about to fly from her lips, though Flora could see this took quite the effort as Shona's mouth was pinched and her eyes mere slits as she regarded the two men. No doubt remembering that she was to be paid handsomely for this from the production company, Shona simply said, "There's teas and coffees over there. Juice if you want it," before retreating to the back of the pub where she couldn't be called upon to provide more alcoholic libations before the lunch hour.

"They only do house white and red in here. Though I could quite do with a sweet sherry myself," Hilda May spoke up, blushing bright red as Evangelista took her hand in his and kissed it.

"Now that is a shame. I've told them they need to up their standards," the show's septuagenarian host said, looking pointedly at Grimes before turning his attention to Betty who couldn't help a schoolgirl giggle as he repeated the same obsequious gesture with her.

As if waiting for her turn, Jean was bobbing up and

14

down in her seat, evidently completely starstruck. The wait of a few seconds as the man turned to her seemed to be too long, however, and she shot up out of her chair and offered her hand ready before Evangelista had even clocked her.

"Oh! You're keen!" He said with a lascivious wink, bending to kiss Jean's wrinkled hand and spending much longer in the doing than he had with her neighbours.

Jean nodded, apparently having been rendered speechless by the experience.

Flora, too, was speechless but for entirely different reasons.

"So, now that Bruce his here, shall we get started? His usual tardiness has already cost us an hour," Grimes began.

"Suck on it," Flora heard the presenter tell the director under his breath, before he helped himself to a black coffee with four sugars and took the seat next to Jean, much to her evident appreciation.

Seeing the move, and her friend's reaction, astute-as-always Betty piped up, "I hope there's not going to be favourites on this show?"

"Of course not," Grimes' assistant Kirsty was quick to reassure her. A small, bespectacled woman dressed in various shades of brown, she had the slow gait of one who has the world on their shoulders. As yet, she had still to produce even one smile, and Flora wondered if the woman's face was always set in that permanent scowl – to be fair, working for Grimes and with Evangelista as she did, Flora couldn't blame her for her dour demeanour. They were only a little over an hour in, and Flora's mood was already affected by the whole ensemble.

"Well, you make sure there's not," Betty said, in a manner which came out rather threateningly considering they were talking about a craft show.

Ignoring the interruption, Grimes hurried on, "Well, we have some good news on the contestant front actually, since only one of the two other ladies who were scheduled to take part can now make it. Amanda will be joining us tomorrow first thing when we begin properly as she was already busy this weekend when the dates were settled. She won a competition to be on the show and Kirsty tells me she's very excited."

"So, does that mean there's an extra spot?" Jean asked.

"Oh, you needn't worry about that, my dear," Bruce spoke up, furnishing the shopkeeper with his best twinkling beam, his stark white veneers no doubt visible from space, "a bobby dazzler like you will be a shoo-in. I have the last word on contestant choices."

"What's this?" Betty shot off her seat as fast as her eighty-odd years would allow and bent forwards directly in front of the man. Evangelista tipped his head back no doubt in an attempt to make himself appear bigger and more impressive in her critical sight, his toupee sliding slowly backwards as he did so. The hilarious hairpiece was now resting on the back of the man's scalp, the front of his head bald apart from a few combed-over stragglers. Yet again, Flora felt a surge of relief that she'd left her feathered friend at home.

"Now Betty," Flora tried to pour oil on troubled waters, but her friend was having none of it.

"I'll have you know, I'm by far the best..." Betty began, waggling her finger in front of Bruce's face aggressively.

"Now, now," Grimes said, sighing heavily and shooting a glare at Evangelista as if he had let slip a show secret, "you'll have read our contract, no abuse towards production staff. But, as it happens, yes, you're in luck. There are three places left, you three ladies are here. So the numbers are simple." He mopped his head dramatically, as if that had been anything but simple, and the ever-attentive Kirsty furnished him with a glass of iced water. Clearly disgusted by the healthy drink, Grimes handed the untouched glass straight back to his assistant.

Betty sat back down, a smug smile of satisfaction on her face as Evangelista and Jean began whispering between themselves and Hilda May eyed up the bottles of sherry behind the bar. Apparently the usual Yarn Wars stress had begun for her and the habitual cup of Earl Grey would no longer suffice.

Flora herself was about to make a hasty exit when Shona's high-pitched voice came up from the pub's cellar.

And by all accounts, she was highly displeased.

THREE

"I just don't understand what the creeping weirdo was doing down there in the first place," Shona said for the third time, as Flora saw Grimes giving the guilty party – namely Chris the runner – a good talking to as if he was a small boy and not a middle-aged man.

"Well what excuse did he give for being in the cellar?" Flora asked, forcing herself to feign interest in the seemingly small matter which she believed Shona to be blowing out of all proportion.

"Said he got lost on the way to the loos! As if!"

"What's all this?" Adam's sane, grounding voice was like music to Flora's ears in that moment. They had arranged that he would come to collect her at eleven if there had been no sign of her in the tearoom by then – a secret escape plan, if you will.

"I found that skinny weirdo over there…" Shona paused to point for Adam's benefit, "skulking about in the cellar taking photos of random things, the barrels, the stairs, the freezers even."

"Well, ah, I'm sure it was all innocent," Adam lifted a querying eyebrow in Flora's direction and she simply shrugged her shoulders in reply, "but I can have a chat with him if you like?"

"No need," Grimes the director butted into the conversation, "he says he was looking for the loo and then thought he could recommend the place as a location for one of our historical dramas. Shocking lack of alcohol round here though… you call yourself a public house?" And he wandered off again, muttering to himself.

"Historical?" Shona shrieked to his retreating back, "I'll have you know we recently renovated and redecorated this place!"

Adam steered Flora gently to the side, "I can see you've had the perfect morning, love," he whispered.

"Yes, absolutely joyful," Flora whispered back, "and I'd love to leave with you right now, but Jean over there has been cosied up to the show's presenter for the past half an hour, Hilda is desperate for a tipple and Betty has all guns blazing, so I should probably..."

"You aren't their keeper, love, they're all grown women," Adam began as suddenly Bruce Evangelista jumped to his feet and shouted, "Spin me a yarn," and all of the crew and ladies chanted back, "And make it a good one!" as if on autopilot.

"I guess that's one of his catchphrases," Flora whispered, as her husband stared aghast at the flamboyant diva whose wig was coming perilously close to making a run for it.

"Bruce, can we go through the main logistics before you start getting carried away? If you don't mind!" Grimes' booming foghorn of a voice had returned in full force as he tried to get them all back on track. It was a futile effort though, as the ancient performer carried on regardless.

"The show where you've got to be a stickler for the stitches and an artist with the needles," he spread his arms with a flourish.

"Get Set Knit!" The ladies chanted, giggling as if they

were a quarter their age.

"I'm not sure how much more of this I can take," Adam said under his breath.

"Me neither," Flora agreed, as Grimes physically hip bumped Bruce out of the way and took centre stage once more.

"Oy! You know I just had that hip replaced," Evangelista shouted, before realising what he had inadvertently admitted and stalking off like a petulant child.

"So," Grimes began quickly while he had everyone's attention, leaving Flora and Adam stuck at the far end of the bar with any chance of a swift escape now having disappeared, "let's just go quickly through the rounds and the rules."

"We watch this every week," Betty spoke up, indignant that her status as superfan was being questioned.

"Ah, yes, Mrs. um…"

"Bentley, you can call me Betty."

"Right you are, but you'll find it's quite a different experience being on this side of the camera."

"Young Amy says she'll pop round and do my make-up and give me a nice purple rinse and set," Betty bit back, angered that her appearance which she took so much pride in was being questioned.

"What? Oh, no, no, no. I meant the way we do things not how you'll look in front of the cameras. It isn't quite as… simple as it appears on the tele. For example, we provide the knitting needles so that everyone is equal."

"You do what?" Jean seemed to come out of her reverie for a moment, "But I was planning on using my gold-plated lucky needles. They're from Italy, you know."

"Pfff, Italian is so last season," Hilda May quipped back, having somehow snuck behind the bar and helped herself when Shona's attention was otherwise diverted.

"Yes, no lucky needles, favourite yarns, family heirloom patterns," Grimes shook his head, his voice a bored monotone, "and, as another example, in the freestyle round, we will take a shot of you beginning your knits, and then hand you half-completed projects to claim as your own, just to save some filming time. Kirsty already arranged with the lovely pregnant lady across the road to provide some of her exceptional work, so we can give at least one of you that… shame she's not able to participate herself."

"What? You want me to pass Rosa's stitches off as my own?" Betty shrieked, even her usually impenetrable hairspray almost unable to prevail against the force of her violent head shaking, "This can't be, it's all done fair and square on the programme."

"Kirsty, can you explain? I need a cigarette," Grimes left his mouselike assistant to deal with the furious pensioner, and Flora did not envy her the task.

"Well," Kirsty began, "we need you to accept these things if you wish to participate. It's all there in the contract, ah let me see…" she scrolled through her electronic tablet until she brought up the document in question, "Yes, here it is. Paragraph three point B, 'contestants must be prepared to accept variations, alterations, additions and compromises to their own work,' so if you wish to take part you have to agree to us asking you to drop a stitch or… well, there are no exceptions I'm afraid, not after what happened last season."

"Which we don't mention or the legal team will have our behinds!" Grimes bellowed from the doorway, where he was surrounded by a cloud of nicotine smoke.

"Drop a stitch? Deliberately?" Betty clutched at her heart as if she'd been mortally wounded.

"Indeed. For the sake of the show's viewers, to raise tension and increase excitement."

"She's raised tension all right," Adam whispered.

Flora didn't have a chance to answer as the room was filled with the sound of Betty's very vocal diatribe. Both angry and disappointed, the older woman didn't hold back her thoughts on the matter as she scraped back her chair, took hold of Hilda May by the elbow so pulling her to her feet, and left without a backward glance.

"Well, I, ah, do you know of anyone else who'd be willing to participate?" Kirsty asked a shocked Flora.

Flora shook her head, looking pointedly at Jean who could usually be relied on to come up with something. There would be no help in that quarter, though, as the shopkeeper was now ensconced in a back corner with Bruce Evangelista, apparently oblivious to the goings on around them.

"It's a small village, mainly made up of the over sixty," Adam said sagely, "given the amount of hysteria there's been in certain groups regarding the show's arrival, you'll find willing participants quick enough. Perhaps ask the vicar's wife for some contact details, the vicarage is just up the road."

And with that he and Flora made a quick and quiet exit. This was not their mess to deal with and for that the pair were extremely grateful.

FOUR

The autumn sun shone warmly as Flora and Reggie made their way to the vicarage the next morning, the little parrot taking great interest in the fallen leaves in their russets and golds. Swooping down to pin them with his talons, he inspected them as if he expected to have landed some great treasure. Finding they were neither edible nor worth playing with, Reggie dismissed them all as a "Stupid git," and flew ahead to where he had spotted a small group beside the duck pond on the green.

"Reggie! Come back please!" Flora called, but as per usual she might as well have saved her breath as the wayward bird ignored her request and headed straight into the action.

Harry had phoned Flora the night before, exhausted from dealing with an irate Betty, asking for Flora's view on the whole debacle. Flora had been honest and told him that she felt Betty was well within her rights to be upset. There'd been no previous inkling that the behind the scenes truths of the show were so far from what was presented in the final cut. The fact that Betty wasn't simply being dramatic and had good cause to feel disappointed had therefore spurred her husband on to take it up with the programme's director, and Flora could see the pair now deep in a rather heated discussion. Thankfully, neither Betty nor Hilda were anywhere to be seen and Flora slipped past without either of the men noticing.

Her elusive sidling was short-lived, however, as Reggie had spotted a stranger and was keen to introduce himself.

"She's a corker!" The bird squawked, landing on the head of a tall, greying, middle-aged woman who shrieked and started hopping up and down on the spot.

"I am so sorry," Flora spoke loudly as she ran over, by which time Reggie had made it to the newcomer's shoulder and was nuzzling her neck as if they were best buddies.

"Reginald Parrot!" Flora moved as if to scoop the bird up but he took to flight instead, shrieking, "You old trout! Get out of it!" and garnering them the attention of all assembled.

Ignoring him, Flora focused her attention on the shaken woman in front of her, "I'm really sorry. He likes to make new friends but he's not very subtle about it."

"Don't worry, I actually like birds. I just got a shock, that's all," she smiled and held out her hand, "Amanda Brookes, I'm a contestant on Yarn Wars."

"Flora Bramble-Miller. I own a tearoom up on the estate," Flora always liked to play down her role in the village when making introductions. Her old feelings of inadequacy rearing their ugly heads from time to time.

"Well, I must say this is a beautiful area, I've never been north of York before, barely left Winchester in fact."

"Yes, we're very lucky to live here. It's the last English county before Scotland, so we do get some questionable weather, but other than that…"

Their introductions were cut short then as all hell seemed to break loose just to the left of the two women. Turning swiftly in that direction, afraid that Harry and Grimes might have come to blows, it was instead the show's presenter, Bruce Evangelista who was hollering and pointing towards the duck pond. Moving closer as they all were, Flora followed the direction of the man's finger to see a bright green ball of feathers, hovering above the expanse of water and holding a small furry animal in his beak.

At least, it looked like a small creature. Until Flora noticed that the man's head was looking decidedly bald...

"The toupée," Flora muttered, horrified.

"Give that back, you mangy seagull," Bruce waved his fist in the air ineffectually.

"Any fool knows seagulls aren't green and yellow," Harry said, apparently seeing the man for the first time, "hey, don't I know you?"

"Well, I am famous. Perhaps you've seen one of my world class productions?"

Harry pursed his lips and sucked in his cheeks as if deep in thought.

"That bird should've been shot long ago," Edwina Edwards piped up. Apparently she had been talking to the cameraman, no doubt trying to get her face on screen.

Flora was about to give the woman a piece of her mind, when Amanda spoke up instead, "What an awful thing to say!"

Apparently shocked to be so chastised by a visitor, Edwina went bright red and clamped her mouth shut.

In the moments this had taken to play out, Reggie had done two laps above the pond and, to Flora's horror, now launched the unlucky headpiece into the water, where it half-floated like a bloated vole.

"Chocks away!" he squawked happily, basking in the attention, "Cows loose!"

"You little flying rat!" Evangelista hollered.

"Reginald Parrot!" It was Flora who was squawking now. She had no idea what to do for the best. Reggie however had no such indecision, and was doing a victory lap over their heads screeching, "Good riddance!"

"Perhaps he thought it was a mouse or something," Amanda said kindly.

Flora was too shocked by her pet's behaviour to reply.

Grimes couldn't seem to contain his mirth, seeing the embarrassment of his colleague as an apparently hilarious interlude in a so-far boring day. It was Kirsty who was left to say, "Someone will have to retrieve it. Chris? Chris?"

The show's runner appeared from the direction of the church hall. Flora had no idea what he'd been doing up there and assumed that perhaps the crew had been given use of the facilities.

"What now?" He snapped, as if helping wasn't his exact job description and he had been interrupted doing something much more important.

To be fair, Flora thought to herself, *rescuing wigs from ponds probably isn't what he signed up for.*

With no long poles to hand, and given the drowning article was almost in the centre of the water anyway, Chris took off his shoes and socks and rolled up his trousers with only half a dozen or so grumbled expletives to accompany the action. All assembled watched him with a mixture of apprehension and glee – well, just Grimes seemed to be gleeful, everyone else was mesmerised in the way that you can't take your eyes off a car crash.

Landing on Flora's shoulder, Reggie seemed very

pleased with himself, preening his feathers in response to a job well done.

"We'll talk about this later," Flora hissed, as if warning a child and received the admonition of "Bad bird!" as reply.

It was all going so well... until it wasn't. Apparently the pond wasn't the same level throughout and took a sudden dip into much deeper water a few feet in. Who knew? Certainly, none of the villagers had ever waded through it to find out. Unfortunately Chris was all too aware now, as his footing slipped with the sudden change in depth and the poor man lurched forwards into the water. His whole body disappeared for a brief second until he reemerged, soaking wet and cursing.

"Sleep with the fishes!" Reggie screeched merrily.

It was at that point that Flora beat a very hasty retreat up to the vicarage, before either Bruce or Chris decided to ring the silly parrot's neck.

"Pets, such a joy," she muttered to herself as she kept her head down and held onto the culprit so that he couldn't fly off again.

"Love me tender…" Reggie chirped away to himself contentedly. So far it had been the best day since yesterday!

FIVE

Flora knocked on the vicarage door with rather more force than usual, desperate to get into the welcoming safety that the home offered and away from the angry shouts which she could still hear coming from behind her. It wasn't Sally who opened the door, however, but rather a very upset looking Lily, who brushed straight past Flora without even a hello.

"Is everything okay with her? Is she put out to not be on the knitting show?" Flora asked Sally who hovered in the hallway wringing her hands.

"Secrets and lies!" Reggie screeched, picking up on the strange atmosphere. That was the final straw for Flora, whose nerves were shot with his ongoing antics. She marched straight to the rarely used dining room and shut the bird in there, ignoring his indignant protests which could still be heard even when the two women were sat in the kitchen.

"So, about Lily," Flora prompted while they waited for the kettle to boil, "is it the knitting? Does she feel left out?"

"No, not at all, didn't even mention it in fact," Sally replied slowly, clearly picking her words carefully, " I don't think she has the headspace for something so frivolous right now."

"Oh?" Flora replied, her interest piqued and concern rising for her friend.

"I can't really say, I'm sorry Flora but she spoke to me in confidence."

"I completely understand. Maybe you could suggest something I could do to help though, without actually giving anything away."

Sally thought on that for a few moments, tapping her fingers on the wooden table, "Yes, I think that might be beneficial actually. Do you think you could go up to the farm? And take Adam with you? Just a social visit."

Slightly surprised by the latter half of the request, as Adam was one of the least social people she knew, Flora nodded, "Absolutely, we can head up there when we've closed up this evening. Do you think it would be appropriate to take Naomi?"

"Ah, maybe not. Could she come here and help with the girls?"

"Of course."

And so it was decided and they turned their attention to the upcoming afternoon tea party to celebrate Sally's complete remission from the brain cancer that had propelled the vicarage family's life into upheaval. The event was to be a celebration for the whole Marshall clan and all their neighbours, and to plan something so meaningful brought a happy glow to Flora's heart.

The guest list was finalised and a pot of tea consumed as Flora went on to describe the scene Reggie had caused when the pair arrived. Sally couldn't help but laugh, having already had the pleasure of meeting Bruce Evangelista first thing that morning when he had knocked to ask if they had a spare bedroom he could use as a dressing room for the duration of filming. Shocked by the unexpected request from the stranger on her doorstep and still in her dressing gown, Sally had given him the keys to the church hall and asked James to check on the place when he was finished morning prayers in the church.

"He does seem rather vain," Sally whispered, as if they were sharing secrets in class, "and I did look him up on the internet afterwards, just to check he is who he said he was, and did you know his real name is actually Barry Evans?"

"No!" Flora's eyes bulged wide at the juicy gossip.

"Yes, that whole fancy accent is a fake. He's as Welsh as they come! Apparently he received a rather large fine for tax evasion last year, as well as a bill for the outstanding amount so he's having to take any work he can to avoid jail time. There was also a more worrying article that he's been preying on older women trying to leech their money off them."

"Wow, no wonder he wants to keep that secret," Flora said.

"I mean, it was in the tabloids so don't take my word for it," Sally whispered, as the kitchen door opened and both ladies jumped apart as if they'd been caught meddling.

"Ah, I just went into the dining room to fetch my satchel," James looked rather perplexed as he was drowned out by the parrot on his shoulder screeching, "Get out of it! Somebody else! Stupid git!"

"I think we'd better take that as our cue to leave," Flora said, sighing heavily, "come on mister, you've caused enough trouble for one morning."

As if he had no idea what she might be referring to, the cheeky green bird flew to Flora's arm, "My Flora, so cosy."

"It's a good job I love you," she whispered as they said their goodbyes and Flora prayed she could get back to Front Street without being spotted by the TV team.

Opting to avoid the direct route and instead to hug as much as possible to the side of the building, Flora crept along, all the while tapping on Reggie's beak to keep him quiet. A shrill sound from her left caused her to stop abruptly, thankfully still in the shadows, as she spotted a familiar figure in a group of trees that stood to the side of the church hall. Unable to help herself when she realised he was engaged in an animated conversation, his broad Welsh accent clear now, Flora listened in as Bruce – or Barry as he really was – railed at his agent, giving him the proverbial both barrels. Apparently this gig was below him, it wasn't going to propel his career anywhere. No, it absolutely wasn't already on the skids, and he certainly wasn't headed into obscurity without the role. Retirement? You've gotta be joking and no he wasn't lucky to be given the job in the first place. Clearly it wasn't just his accent that was fake, Flora noted, but also the man's enthusiasm for the television show. She wondered how many of his colleagues knew he felt the whole thing was "beneath him" as Evans was now bemoaning.

Not wanting to be caught, Flora hurried on her way, glad that Betty and Hilda were no longer part of the whole farce. Jean though, now she was a worry, and Flora made a note to call into the shop later and try to dissuade her friend from making a fool of herself with the fake philanderer. An easy task? Flora doubted it, but she felt she must try.

So much for not getting involved in it all, she thought to herself, as she finally rounded the corner to the main street and released the angry bundle of feathers who made his feelings very clear.

Flora tuned out the parrot's litany of her perceived failings and hurried back along to the tearoom, her mind whirring with thoughts of Lily and Jean, of Betty, Harry and Hilda. Despite her protestations to the contrary, Flora was deeply protective of her little community and did feel a personal responsibility for everyone in Baker's Rise.

If Yarn Wars threatened their peace, then perhaps the show needed a reason to leave the village sooner rather than later.

SIX

After a quick meal of corned beef and potato pie with chunky chips, Flora and Adam dropped a sulking Naomi at the vicarage and promised to be back as quickly as possible. Clearly something had happened at school, but despite prompts and bribes, the teenager steadfastly refused to discuss it with them. Reggie – who was still in disgrace – had been left at the manor house to contemplate his earlier actions. Or at least to doze on his perch after stuffing in half a banana and four huge grapes which their daughter had fed him on her return from school. They were as thick as thieves, those two.

"So, tell me again what we're meant to be doing. You're sure it wouldn't be considered interfering?"

Adam asked as they drove to Jean's shop.

"Well, we're going to make sure our friend doesn't make a mistake with a geriatric fraudster and then we're heading to the farm. I'm not sure what we'll find there exactly, but I'm sure we can handle it between us."

"Hmm," was all her husband replied as they pulled up outside Baker's Rise Essential Supplies to find Betty just leaving the store.

"How are you doing?" Flora asked, in the way you might speak to someone who has just suffered a bereavement, sympathetic head tilt and all.

"I'm grand," Betty's tone was defensive, "why wouldn't I be? I always had my suspicions that programme was all fake."

Flora and Adam shared a look but said nothing as the older woman continued.

"And I've told little Tina here if she sees that grimy director she's to nip his ankles!"

"I'm not sure that's..." Adam began, but Betty had already stalked off, the terrier trotting along to match her speed.

Their welcome in the small shop was hardly warm either, as Jean seemed rather annoyed to have more customers. The shopkeeper's hair was fashioned in large, plastic curlers, almost hidden under a silk scarf, and her face greasy with what must have been industrial strength face cream.

"I was just closing up early," she said, "so if you can be quick please!"

"Oh! Doing something nice?" Flora asked, a sinking feeling in the pit of her stomach.

"A date actually," the shopkeeper's cheeks flushed, "I'm cooking for someone."

"Anyone special?"

Jean peered at them through calculating eyes, "No, just an old friend."

Once again, Flora and Adam shared a private look as they pretended to need more milk and sugar. The sound of a tin hitting the floor from somewhere near the back of the shop startled Flora, and Adam urged her quickly to the till, not keen to come face to face with Jean's grumpy cat, Smudge.

"I'd bet my best handbag that it's Evans she's meeting," Flora said when they were back in the car, the noise of the bolts locking and the closed sign on the shop door turned before they'd even walked across the narrow pavement. She'd already told her husband about Evangelista's true identity. Adam had reminded her that most old performers, and a lot of young ones, use stage names, but Flora still felt it was shady. Especially combined with the other things she'd heard about the man. If he was truly on his uppers then it would make sense that he'd target Jean, a trusting woman in her seventies who clearly had eyes for him. A business owner and widow to boot.

"Well, she's a grown adult who can make her own choices," Adam said, though even he looked concerned.

It was already dusk by the time they got to the farm, the autumn sun setting low in the sky over the fields with a final burst of oranges and pinks. To say the farmer's wife was not her usual welcoming self would be a huge understatement. Indeed, it was only by pretending she had an urgent matter to discuss that Flora got them an invite into the farmhouse at all. The usually hospitable couple appeared to have battened down the hatches and weren't open to unexpected social visits. In fact, Stan was nowhere to be seen at all. His usual chair by the open fire was empty, the logs left unattended to burn down to embers. Even Bertie the collie seemed desolate, lying on the rug where his master's slippered feet normally rested.

"So, what was it exactly?" Lily asked as they took a seat at the farmhouse kitchen table. For once, there was no smell of baking, no offer of hot drinks or tasty treats. Instead, the farmer's wife looked pale and washed out, her apron dirty and her face splattered with what looked like mud.

Flora couldn't help her worried expression as she asked, "Is everything okay, Lily?"

Their friend's mouth opened as if to offer some immediate pat response, before closing again. This happened a couple of times as they sat silently, before Lily's face crumpled, her hands quickly coming up to cover her tears.

"Lily, what is it? What can we do to help?" Flora jumped from her seat and moved across to her friend, bending down to put an arm around her shoulders.

"Shall I get Stan?" Adam asked, clearly uncomfortable, "Is he home?"

"He is, but he won't come through," Lily moved one hand so that they could hear her, "he lies in that bedroom night and day, no energy, no motivation to do anything."

"Is he ill?" Flora asked gently. The parish council had yet to approve another doctor for the village, having had their hands burned last time, so she was aware everyone now had to go to Alnwick or Morpeth to be seen. Given how busy Stan always was on the farm, perhaps he hadn't been able to make time.

"Aye, but not in the way you mean. I got him a phone consultation the other day. At my wits' end I was, struggling to do all the farm chores myself."

"What? No, Lily that's too much now all your seasonal workers have left." *No wonder the woman looks exhausted,* Flora thought. "Couldn't you ask Laurie to help?" He was their godson after all.

"No, he's a lovely lad but what with Rosa's pregnancy complications I don't want to be a burden on him."

"I'm sure he wouldn't think that," Adam said gently, "but what did the doctor say about Stan?"

"Depression, he thinks," Lily spoke through renewed sobs and paused for a moment to compose herself, "my Stan's not been right since that murder up here at last year's autumn fayre. Then there's me opening the shop in the village, which is great for money coming in, but left him alone to cope up here. I think it started out as loneliness, and then… well, he wouldn't talk about it for months, just kept snapping at me and fobbing me off as men do. Now he rarely leaves the bedroom and I'm just… I mean, I don't know what to…"

"Shh," Flora comforted her, "we can work something out. Perhaps something for all the men in the village. Eh, Adam?"

"Of course," her husband agreed quickly, "we could all use a bit of camaraderie, couldn't we? I'll speak to James Marshall and Christopher Cartwright and see what we can arrange. In the meantime, I can spare some time to help you up here, Lily."

"Are you sure? You don't have to."

"Absolutely. You know, when I was in the force we saw a lot of cases of anxiety and depression. PTSD even. Men who had so much pride they didn't want to admit to it. I took a few courses and can bring you the booklets if you like? Maybe when I'm up here, I could have a chat with Stan over a cuppa, in the bedroom if he wants."

Flora could not have loved her husband more in that moment. Emotions, especially discussing feelings, were not his comfort zone, but to see him willing to help a friend like that filled her with warmth.

"Thank you, both of you," Lily dried her face on her apron, before realising how scruffy it was and taking it off quickly. She took a clean one from the cabinet drawer and put it on, "Now, let's put the kettle on."

SEVEN

The morning had not gone as Flora had envisaged – far from it in fact. What was meant to be a tranquil, routine-filled start to the day had turned into a fraught drive to the high school in Alnwick, at the headteacher's request, to collect Naomi who had apparently got into a highly volatile 'discussion' with some of her peers.

"Why didn't you tell us they'd been bullying you because of The Rise?" Adam asked as they drove home. He and Flora had felt awful hearing this for the first time from Naomi's form teacher today. They had brought their daughter home to talk things through in familiar surroundings not because she had been suspended or anything like that, but clearly the girl still felt she was being punished and so was immediately on the defensive.

"I thought I could handle it," the tearful teenager replied from the back seat, "and I could, until they started calling it a haunted house. I mean, at least get it right! 'It's not a haunted house,' I told them, 'it's a murder magnet.'"

"What?" Flora was horrified, "it's not a murder magnet, Naomi, it's just unfortunately been..." She was interrupted by the sound of Adam's phone ringing through the Bluetooth linked to the car's radio.

"Hello?" Adam asked, impatient to get back to the conversation at hand.

"Adam? It's Jean. Sorry to bother you so early, but could you come round please... urgently."

"Jean, it's Flora. Is everything okay?" It was hardly early, gone ten thirty in fact.

"Yes, yes, nothing to panic about... just a dead body in my bedroom."

"A what?" Flora squeaked.

"See, I told you, murder magnet, that's what Baker's

Rise is," the little voice in the back piped up, earning her a disapproving glare in the rearview mirror from Adam.

"We'll be there in five minutes," he replied.

Naomi was left with Granny Betty whose curiosity was certainly piqued, but Flora didn't have time for hellos let alone explanations as she hurried down the street after her husband. The shop door was already unlocked so they let themselves in and raced up the narrow staircase to Jean's flat above. The curtains were still drawn, leaving the sitting room in an eerie half-light, as the couple found Jean sitting calmly on the settee, stroking the large bundle of fur that was Smudge the cat. The feisty feline hissed at the visitors, clearly resenting the interruption in his daily massage schedule, as Jean looked up blankly.

"Jean, are you okay? You called us, and asked us to come round," Flora said, shooting a worried glance at Adam.

"I'll take a look," the former detective said, striding towards the bedroom without a qualm.

"I, ah, my head hurts, feels groggy," Jean said, dumping the cat unceremoniously from her lap and standing, rubbing both temples as if to clear the brain fog.

"You mentioned a dead body?" Flora pressed.

"What? Oh yes. In the bedroom there," she led the way to join Adam who was staring at the large, naked form of none other than Bruce Evangelista, or Barry Evans as he had been born. Lying flat on his back on the double bed, a pile of vomit beside him, the late presenter of Yarn Wars was decorated with a set of gold-plated knitting needles, driven straight into his chest in the area of the man's heart. No blood was visible, though.

"Stand back, I'll phone this in. Don't touch anything," Adam said, stepping out of the room."

"Eugh, what a sight," Jean whispered, before rushing from the room accompanied by the sounds of her throwing up a minute later.

Flora wasn't sure if the reaction was because the man was displayed in all his gory glory or dead, but she certainly felt her own breakfast might make a reappearance at any moment. Oddly, the main thing that caught her eye in that moment was that Evans' fake tan only went as far down as his neck. Other than his equally orange hands, the rest of him was a pasty white colour.

Flora joined her friend, bringing her a glass of water and rubbing Jean's back. The poor woman was still in her clothes from the night before, make-up smeared across her aged face and her best dress all dishevelled.

"Right, they'll be here in half an hour from Morpeth," Adam said, closing the door on the room in question and joining the women in the small kitchen area, "let's have a cup of sweet tea, shall we? Then you can tell me all about it, Jean."

"Yes, good idea, and maybe some paracetamol for my pounding head. But first, there's ah, something worse I have to show you."

"Worse than a dead body?" Flora's eyes were wide and she shot another worried glance at her husband.

"Aye lass, come this way," Jean led them into the second bedroom, no more than a box room really, and flicked on the light switch.

Flora had no words.

Nor, it would seem, did her husband.

They both stood there, mouths agape, staring at what could only be described as a shrine to the man lying dead in the room next door. With newspaper cuttings and magazine articles, marketing posters and theatre programmes going back fifty years or so, the room was dedicated to the life and work of Bruce Evangelista.

"I know, it's a bit of a shock," Jean whispered.

That had to be the understatement of the year, and still Flora couldn't quite think of the right thing to say. Was there even a right thing under the circumstances?

"Ah, this might take some explaining," Adam left the room, a noticeable tremor running the length of him as if the obsessive dedication to the television star had given him the creeps more than any murder scene could.

Jean began to sob quietly and Flora put a comforting arm around her friend's shoulder, "Don't worry, we'll get it all sorted. Let's have a cuppa, eh? Then you can tell us all about it."

Inside though, Flora wasn't sure she wanted to hear the whole sordid tale. She'd much rather be back in her cosy tearoom with Tanya, or in front of the log fire at Betty's. Anywhere, really, apart from in a small flat with yet another dead body and another neighbour likely to be prime suspect for the murder.

Apparently, according to her daughter, it was just another average day in Baker's Rise!

EIGHT

"So, tell me how last night played out. From the beginning," Adam said once the two women were seated on Jean's small sofa, he himself pacing the little room in impatient steps as if he couldn't rest until he knew what had happened.

"Well, Bruce came round for dinner," Jean gestured to the small table, where two half-eaten plates of beef bourguignon sat untouched since the night before, "and that's all I can remember. I woke up this morning, still fully dressed, on the floor beside the table there with Smudge using me as his personal hot water bottle."

"There must be something more," Adam pushed. "Did

anyone else join you? Did you make the food yourself? How much did you drink? Forgive me, but you seem quite hungover. I know you may be embarrassed to tell us if things got… amorous between the two of you, but it's best to tell us now, before McArthur and Timpson get here."

"Amorous? Oh! Certainly not!" Jean's voice was full of all the indignation she felt, "The man was fully clothed the last time I saw him. I cooked, he brought the wine. We flirted, we began eating, then… blackout." Jean wiped the tears that were falling in silent grief that the man she had had a crush on since her teenage years was now dead. And not only that, but murdered in her own bedroom by all accounts.

"And you have a sore head?" Adam asked, tapping his chin with his finger, immune to the show of emotion as he reverted to the stoically implacable demeanour of his former profession.

"I do, I feel hungover, but I must've only drunk a glass. Very nice English wine it was."

"And where is the bottle? And the glasses you used?" Adam asked.

Jean stood up and went to the table, then to the kitchen, even looking in the bin, her gait lethargic, "I have no idea. That's strange."

"Hmm," was all Adam said as they heard sirens in the distance.

It was well after lunch before the body was taken away for a post mortem to ascertain cause of death. The knitting needles had been symbolic, so the detectives thought. A gesture which evidently meant a lot to the murderer. The fact that they were Jean's lucky needles – not so lucky in Bruce's case – didn't look good for the kindly shopkeeper. Nor the fact that the deceased was discovered on Jean's own bed. Then had come the shrine room – a shocker to all assembled, as you might imagine.

Adam had advocated for their friend, though, suggesting that it sounded like she had been drugged, the missing wine bottle and glasses also supporting that theory. So Timpson had been charged with taking Jean to the health centre in Morpeth to have bloods taken to see if she had any sedative in her system, whilst the forensics team worked in the bedroom. Bruce's clothes were bagged up and the whole room dusted for prints, as were the dining table and kitchen counters. Flora hadn't stayed once her friend had left, though Adam was keen to 'support' the investigation and so hung around, even placating the yowling housecat with a tin of tuna to get the miserable creature on side.

"Grandad Harry says he's a washed up old has-been who passed his prime decades ago," Naomi declared once they were back in the tearoom, having shared the whole grisly tale with Tanya.

"Well he's a dead has-been now, so have some respect," Tanya replied, though she smiled at the girl, no doubt admiring her spirit.

"Yes, apparently Harry remembers him from some scandal on Blackpool pier in the eighties, when he was first done for tax fraud I think," Flora added, "not a nice man by all accounts. I've no idea what Jean saw in him."

"Well, I guess he was much more handsome back in his prime when she started fancying him," Tanya said, and opened her mouth as if to expand on her thoughts before remembering Naomi was still with them and instead adding, "there's nowt as strange as folk." A saying she had learnt from Betty.

The bell above the tearoom door rang, alerting Reggie

who had been guarding the empty bookshop in Adam's absence, "Watch Out! Hide It All!" the little parrot screeched, flying through to protect the women.

"Agh!" The new arrival brought her arm up to shield her face from the flapping wings of the small but mighty protector.

"Desist, silly bird!" Tanya said.

"Come on Reggie, let's go and play," Naomi said, going through to the book nook with the parrot hot on her heels.

"My No Me," he screeched, not even sparing a glance backwards to the other women under his supposed care.

"I'm so sorry," Flora said, "please do have a seat."

Amanda Brookes managed a half smile as she chose the table nearest the door, no doubt so she could make a quick escape if the overzealous parrot made a reappearance, "Not at all, I'm sure he's just... territorial."

"Tanya, this is Amanda, one of the Yarn Wars contestants," Flora made the introductions as Tanya fetched a menu.

"I suppose there's no filming today," Tanya blurted.

Subtle, Flora thought, *very subtle.*

"No, there's apparently been an accident with one of the production team," Amanda shrugged, clearly not in possession of all the grisly facts, and Flora smiled overly brightly to compensate for Tanya's slip up.

"Well, it'll give you a chance to look around and get your bearings," Flora said, taking the woman's order for a cappuccino and some carrot cake.

Peace reigned in the little tearoom for all of three minutes before the bell above the door tinkled once again and this time it was Betty and Hilda May who rushed in out of the blowy autumn weather, both clasping their plastic rain hoods under their chin, "So, you tell Hilda here everything you told me about the latest murder," Betty demanded of Flora before she had even taken her coat off let alone sat down.

Flora sank her head into her hands, her elbows already conveniently resting on the front counter, before plastering another smile on her face and welcoming her latest customers.

"What murder is this?" Amanda asked, visibly shaken, half out of her seat already as if the gruesome act may well have taken place in this very building.

"Ah, well," Flora tried to think of a way to downplay the truth without actually fibbing. She needn't have worried though, as Tanya had her back as always.

"That jazzy geriatric bloke, the loud one with the fake hair all mutton dressed as beef. He's been offed in the corner shop," Tanya eagerly shared the local gossip.

"Lamb," Flora corrected on autopilot, "it's mutton dressed as lamb."

Other than that, she had nothing.

NINE

It was much later that evening when Adam reappeared back at the manor house. Flora, Naomi and Reggie had long since eaten and the two women were snuggled up in their pyjamas watching 'Mamma Mia'. Reggie, too, was engrossed in the musical, squawking "Here we go again," whenever the phrase came up. Flora and Adam had spotted Naomi's love of musical theatre early on in her stay and had taken her to a couple of west end shows during their visit to London. The look on the teenage girl's face when she was sitting in the grand theatre for the first time was a memory which Flora would always cherish.

"Long day?" Flora asked her husband as she slipped out of the cosy upstairs family room, "Come down to the kitchen, I've kept your lasagne warm."

"Thanks love, aye it's a thinker that's for sure. I mean, it's obvious Jean was being framed, but it might be tricky pinning down the culprit."

"Is Jean back home?"

"Staying with Hilda May. Her flat's a crime scene so no entry there yet. They've only let her back until the results of the blood test are confirmed tomorrow morning. If there's no sedative in her system proving she was conked out for the whole event then she'll likely be arrested. I suppose they could go with the line that Jean sedated herself after committing the act, and of course that ghoulish room of hers won't help her case," Adam shuddered, "but... well, we'll have to hope more evidence comes to light before then."

"Poor Jean," Flora bent to take the dish out of the oven as Adam poured himself a beer from the fridge, "I mean, she obviously idolised the man so it's going to hit her hard."

"Aye, I don't think it's quite sunk in yet. Once we'd got everything we could from the crime scene, I went with McArthur to speak to that director of the knitting programme. Seemed a sensible place to start taking statements with the people who actually worked with the bloke on the daily."

"Grimes?"

"That's the one. Awful chap, not an ounce of sympathy, just wanted to know when they could get back on track with filming. Apparently there was no love lost between him and Evans and that was no secret amongst the group. I suggested they might want to let this shoot go completely, given the village ladies have already walked out, and get on their way as soon as McArthur gives them permission to leave the village."

"Definitely the best option, I would say. It's been a bad omen all round, that stupid TV show."

"Good riddance!" Reggie added, flying into the kitchen at the end of their conversation.

"Is there any supper?" Naomi asked, yawning as she followed the bird in.

"You two are like two peas in a pod," Flora hugged the girl.

"Two peas in a pod!" Reggie echoed delightedly, sure it must mean an extra serving of blueberries was in his near future.

A midnight call was the last thing the Bramble-Millers either expected or needed, but nevertheless was what they got, with Adam rushing out to the farm on hearing Lily's distress over an intruder. He had already spoken to the farmer's wife earlier that day to apologise for not being able to make it up to help at the farm due to an 'unforeseen incident.' On hearing the sirens from a distance as they entered Baker's Rise that morning, Lily had had more than an inkling that another murder might have occurred in their small village, hence her panic now.

Even Stan, it seemed, had been roused to action by the bellowing of the cows in the shed heralding the arrival of a nighttime trespasser, though when Adam arrived to join the search there was no one to be found. Thankfully, Lily had also called Pat Hughes, whose police dog, Frank, was soon on the case, rooting out a man hiding in the hay loft.

"So he's in police custody?" Flora asked at breakfast the next morning as her husband yawned around his spoonful of cereal.

"Wish I could say that, love, but no. They took him at

his word that he was scoping out a location for a future television production, checked his ID with Grimes and let the man go. He did get a warning for trespassing, but since no harm was done their hands are tied. Much bigger fish to fry at the moment, what with the murder investigation and everything."

"But shouldn't Chris be a suspect for the killing? I mean, as the show's runner he had plenty of opportunity to have a run in with Evans. Maybe an old score to settle there, though I'm pretty sure they said he was new to the team. Maybe he has some backstory they could look into."

"I agree, love, but apparently he's been ruled out of the murder investigation as he and the assistant, Kirsty, are each other's alibi. Bit of a tryst going on if you know what I mean," her husband's expression remained dour, no hint of levity in his tone, so Flora could tell what he thought of that flimsy defence.

"And now here he is skulking about up at the farm. And you saw how Shona found him in the pub cellar, didn't you?" Flora continued, "He used the same excuse then too. Shifty if you ask me. And as for dating Kirsty, what a strange pairing... Oh! Maybe he's a journalist? Yes! That could be it, don't you think? Writing an article on the 'murder village.'"

"Well, that's possible, love, but then why would he be here with the TV crew? Good ideas, though, I'll mention them to McArthur at this morning's briefing in the church hall. They've set up base there for now."

Any further discussion of the matter was halted by the arrival of their daughter and parrot, so Flora had to say a quick goodbye to Adam as she was driving Naomi to school and then heading straight to the tearoom.

"Any more trouble at school, you tell them I'll set Reggie on them," Adam joked, earning him a tut of disapproval from his wife.

"Maybe I could come in, do an assembly about the truth of the matte..." Flora began only to be quickly cut off by her daughter.

"No! Flora please, that'd be so embarrassing!" Naomi rolled her eyes.

If Flora had kept track of everything that the teenager found embarrassing, she'd have filled a notebook by now.

"Well, try not to react, Don't bite back to their taunts," was the advice she did give, "they're just looking for a reaction."

Naomi nodded and smiled, but Flora had the

impression the girl was simply humouring her, not helped when Reggie called her a "stupid old trout" as they were walking to the car.

And this is why you should never work with children or animals, Flora thought as she started the engine.

TEN

The results were in and it looked like Jean was in the clear since her blood and urine tests had shown positive for Rohypnol, a strong sedative often used nefariously. There was still a slight doubt that she may have administered it to herself as some kind of warped cover up, but in that regard the spare room dedicated to her decades-long crush on Bruce Evangelista had actually worked in the shopkeeper's favour, since McArthur couldn't then think of why Jean would want to kill the man. Especially not when the elderly resident finally had him, alive and well, in her own home. No motive meant an unlikely suspect in that detective's book and so Jean was allowed back into her flat, provided she stayed in the village for further questioning if needed. Of course, this raised the question of how the killer entered the shop and went up to the flat. Even working on the assumption the murderer was confident the sedative secreted in the wine would've worked, Adam himself had heard Jean lock up for the night and so could offer no suggestion as to how the killer then managed to get in and out without detection.

"Couldn't she have killed him for refusing her advances?" Timpson spoke up when it was just he, McArthur and Adam back at the church hall, blushing brightly at the subject matter.

"I can hardly see him refusing, can you?" McArthur snapped, "Given what we know of the man's previous liaisons – of which there have been many. One simple internet search shows a bevy of broken hearts from John o' Groats to Land's End dating back to the seventies."

"Well, it's worth considering every avenue," Timpson bit back, and Adam was happy to see the lad was finally getting a backbone.

"It is," Adam tried to referee, "but McArthur is right I think, there's no way Barry Evans was going to that flat, dressed to the nines and with a bottle of wine in his pocket, just to reminisce about his years on the variety scene. On that note, McArthur, any word on the bottle or glasses?"

"None yet, though the search team did find a gift bag and card in the deceased's room at the B&B in Witherham, so that's been sent off for fingerprinting. Not much of a message, just 'from an admirer.'"

"So, the wine may have been a gift?" Adam clarified. He could well imagine Barry Evans being a cheapskate who would avoid paying for the contribution he brought to dinner.

"Could've been, since we're assuming that's where the drug was hidden," McArthur sighed and rubbed her temples, "you know, we might as well just set up an actual station here in Baker's Rise. It'd save all the toing and froing every time there's a murder."

"Don't even joke about it," Adam said, "my daughter's already being bullied about the reputation Baker's Rise is getting."

"Oh I'm sorry to hear that, mate," McArthur replied, "right, onwards and upwards. Let's interview the whole lot of them again. See if we've missed anything."

Adam didn't envy them that task, what with the

production team already getting antsy about heading back out into the real world as soon as possible, and made his excuses to head up to the farm and help Lily.

"Did you speak to Stan?" Flora asked when they caught up back at The Rise that evening. She noticed that Adam had dark grey circles under his eyes from the excitement of the night before and prayed they would get a decent night's sleep.

"Only briefly. Took him a cuppa into the bedroom but he wasn't forthcoming with answers. Just listened to my chatter and then I went back out to help with the chores. He had the curtains closed so the room was shrouded in darkness, really felt for the man I did."

Flora knew that a meeting had been arranged for Friday evening at the vicarage, all the men of the village invited. Not to discuss Stan, per se, because that was his own personal story to share if and when he wanted to, but rather to consider forming a social group for the men to come together once a month or even once a fortnight or so to watch a film or to play board games. Anything really, which would give them all a safe space to share if they needed to.

"Did Naomi have a better day?" Adam asked as they

sat at the kitchen table, he with a strong coffee and Flora with a chamomile tea.

The silence with no parrot adding his tuppence worth, and no teenage dramas to listen to either, was eerily quiet and almost prompted the pair to go and investigate.

"Seems to have, she certainly appeared more upbeat when she got home. Asked if the tea party for Sally was still going ahead on Saturday and if she could do anything to help. That reminds me, could you dig the bunting out of the storage cupboard?"

"Of course. This is lovely, isn't it? No surprise phone calls or visits, no crimes or calamities. Just the two of us and…"

"You jinxed it!" Flora whispered as Adam's phone began vibrating on the table next to them.

Her husband muffled a sigh as he answered the call, nodding and grunting at appropriate intervals to the frustration of Flora, who therefore had no idea as to either who was on the other end of the line or what they wanted.

"Post mortem results came in a while ago," Adam said as he ended the 'conversation.'

"And?" Flora prompted, impatient now.

"You're not going to like it, love."

"Me? Why?"

"Well, it turns out that Evans wasn't killed by the knitting needles – just as we suspected, so far so good – but it turns out that he had two hypodermic injection marks in each buttock. Excised tissue underlying these marks contained insulin."

"What does that mean, Adam? Hurry up and tell me why I'm not going to be happy." Flora could feel her anger rising, not that her husband deserved to be the brunt of it but still.

"It means the murderer is likely diabetic or works in a hospital. To have had access to the needles and insulin to give the victim a lethal quantity, you see."

"Yes, and..?"

"Well, McArthur has checked and no one involved in the show is diabetic, nor are any of the villagers who came into contact with Evans or the production team in general. Except one."

"Who is?"

"Harry."

"Naomi, get your coat, we're going to Granny Betty's!"

ELEVEN

Adam still couldn't quite grasp what had necessitated two adults, one teenager and a parrot all squashing into the car and rushing into the village at gone seven in the evening to pay a social call on an innocent man who wasn't even going to be interviewed by the police until the following morning. Flora, however, was adamant that the man who had been like a father to her since she'd arrived in Baker's Rise wasn't going to be taken by surprise when the detectives turned up on his doorstep. He was surprised when Flora turned up, the whole family in tow, but that was by the by.

"I'm just shocked I didn't know he was diabetic," Flora said to Betty when the pleasantries had been dealt with and Harry had taken Adam and Naomi into the back yard to show them the new racing pigeon he'd acquired. Reggie's nosiness had come back to bite him in the beak when he insisted on flying out there with them, all squawks blazing, and had come face to face with a bird at least triple his size and with an attitude to match. Suitably chastened, the parrot had retreated immediately to Flora's lap, where he now lay sulking and arbitrarily screeching, "Stupid jerk!" to no one in particular.

"Why would you, lass?" Betty asked, "We don't air our dirty laundry in public."

The irony and, dare I say it, hypocrisy was not lost on Flora, as she recalled her friend hanging their neighbours' metaphorical laundry out many a time in gossip-filled conversations with the W.I. ladies in the tearoom. Nevertheless, Flora simply nodded and tried to subtly suggest that Harry not mention his previous knowledge of Evans' character.

"It's bad enough he was arguing with Grimes on set that first day by the pond," Flora said, "best not make it worse by letting on to a previous acquaintance with Evans years back."

Betty made a clicking sound with her tongue against her false teeth and peered at Flora through thick rimmed reading glasses, "Are you saying my Harry has something to hide?"

"What? No! That's not what I meant at all," Flora recoiled at the thought.

"Well then, honesty is the best policy," Betty nodded in agreement with herself, setting her curls off bouncing and Flora smothered a sigh behind her china cup.

As it was, it had all been nothing more than a storm in a teacup. McArthur and Timpson had interviewed Harry in the church hall the next morning over tea and biscuits, with Flora insisting that Adam both be present and then report back to her immediately after the event. By all accounts, after only a few minutes clarifying the facts and reassuring themselves that Harry had no murderous intentions towards the deceased or anyone else for that matter, the conversation had then veered off into the territory of racing pigeons. It turned out Timpson's Grandad had many of the feathery flyers back home in Darlington and he himself was a passionate orator on the subject. A fact which gave Adam and McArthur a chance to have a private chat in the chilly church hall kitchen.

"So, what's your gut on this one?" Adam asked.

"Well, I've got my sights on that director, Grimes. Spends most of his days drowning his sorrows in your local boozer, couldn't stand the deceased and has worked on enough medical documentaries and true crime shows over the years to have a workable knowledge of how to kill someone."

"Interesting. I agree he's not likeable by anyone's standards, but how could he have got in and out without being detected? That's what bothers me. The motive may be there, but the means?"

"Well, if we're going that route, then it's your friendly shopkeeper and erstwhile fangirl of the deceased, Jean Sykes, who's back in the spotlight."

"I just don't think she did it. And not because of any personal connection," Adam replied.

"I agree. Perhaps you could call round to check on her with your lady wife, just a social visit of course, and try to work out how the killer got in? Maybe there's something obvious we're missing?"

"Will do. Flora likes any excuse for social visits, believe you me."

McArthur raised her eyebrows, a small smile on her lips at how her once all-professional partner had now become so domesticated, "You've got a good one there, mate."

"I really do," Adam agreed and he meant it.

And so Flora and her husband just happened to be needing more milk right about closing time that evening. And they just happened to offer to help Jean lock up and then it would've been rude to refuse the cup of tea she offered in return.

Of course, Adam had a good check of the bolts on the front door as he closed the shop up for the night – all good there, nothing notable amiss.

"Jean," he asked nonchalantly as they followed their hostess up the narrow staircase to the flat above, "just out of interest, when you came down that morning after the, ah, incident, and unlocked the door ready for our arrival, did you notice anything different? Unusual? I mean, I'm sure the police have already asked but…"

"What? No. I mean, I didn't come downstairs that morning. I felt too groggy to stand up for too long let alone navigate these stairs," Jean replied, oblivious to the import of what she had just said.

Adam shook his head silently at Flora who was looking to him for some sort of clarification and instead disappeared quietly back down to the shop, no doubt to recheck what he had just looked at.

Furnished with a cup of tea and a slice of lemon drizzle cake a few minutes later, the ex-detective tried again, "So, ah, I think the investigating team just assumed you had opened the door to let us in. Given that you didn't, how did the door get unlocked, do you think?"

"Oh! Well, I haven't thought of that. I suppose the killer just let themselves out."

Flora's eyes were wide at the easy way her friend just provided an explanation without obviously registering what exactly the ramifications of that statement were. She left it to Adam to clarify.

"So, Jean, I think you're right, and the shop door was left unlocked by the murderer. Working on that assumption, how do you think they got in through the locked door in the first place? I know you've told McArthur no one else has a key, there's just that one entry point, and the door is double locked with internal bolts. I mean, even Flora and I heard you lock up on the evening in question. I guess what we haven't spoken in detail about is that another visitor arrived after you locked up for the day, the decea... ah, Mr. Evans, for your evening together. Is it possible you were so excited by his arrival that you forgot to lock up after him?"

"Not at all. He was such a gentleman, even made sure I'd locked us in, said he didn't want us to be disturbed," the older woman blushed at this admission.

"So, how could the murderer have gained entry?" Adam pushed, so far back into detective mode now that he didn't even register the hardness in his tone or the brusque nature of his questioning.

Jean looked completely none the wiser, simply fidgeted with the huge ball of wool in a basket by her feet, so Flora tag teamed with her husband to try to eke out some suggestions.

"I mean, I heard Smudge here at the back of the shop knocking something off the shelf when we were in that night. Could he have levered the bolts on the door open?" It was a ridiculous notion and the fact Adam's eyebrows were practically in his hairline reinforced that, but Flora shrugged her shoulders in his direction and focused back on their hostess.

"Oh no, Smudge never ventures downstairs, never once has. He's far too lazy for that. Treats this flat like his castle and me as his adoring servant," Jean gave an indulgent smile towards her pet, who arched his back and stretched his claws in reply from his lofty position on his cat climbing frame.

Flora and Adam shared a pointed look before he spoke again, "So, if it wasn't Mr. Smudge here in the back of the shop, I'm afraid with all the other evidence we already have, that we must assume the person hid in your shop before closing. Probably slipped in when you came upstairs to, ah, put your curlers in or something. They were already in hence no sign of break in. You've already told the police, Jean, that you have no CCTV in the shop. So, the murderer waited till they heard the telltale sounds of you both collapsing before coming upstairs to commit the fatal crime and then they conveniently let themselves out after the murder so your front door was found unlocked by us in the morning."

"You mean they were here the whole time, while I was getting ready, waiting to pounce?" Jean's chin wobbled.

"No need to get upset," Flora went over to hug her friend, "we won't ever mention it again. Will we Adam?" Flora's expression brooked no argument and her husband knew how to reply.

"Of course not. Nothing to worry about Jean, I just need to nip downstairs and, ah, make a phone call."

"Must've been someone strong to haul Evans' fat ass onto that bed," Flora mused as they headed home shortly afterwards.

"Or someone who had taken a drug, adrenaline or something less classy, to boost their strength," Adam replied, "You'd be surprised, love, what someone can achieve with the right – or wrong as it may be – mindset and the help of non-prescription power aids."

"I hadn't thought of that," Flora mused, glad to be heading back to her cosy family and away from thoughts of moving overweight, sweaty men. Genie had kindly offered to babysit whilst she baked some treats for the weekend's afternoon tea party and Flora had the hope of taste-testing a couple before bed.

"Like with the door," Adam continued, unaware his wife's thoughts had now moved to more culinary experiences, "the answer's generally straightforward – with hindsight at least."

"Umhm," Flora agreed, hoping there'd be those mini eclairs she so loved.

TWELVE

Friday dawned dry and crisp with only a slight chill in the air. Flora put the tweed trousers that she'd planned to wear back in the cupboard and opted for a fully lined corduroy dress instead. She had a very busy day planned and so needed something practical. *No reason to not feel stylish though,* she told herself.

"My Flora, so cosy, you sexy beast," the little bird ensconced on her bedspread chirped, no doubt buttering Flora up so that she would take him with her on her errands.

It worked of course. Adam was seeing Naomi onto the school bus and then heading straight up to help on the farm whilst Flora's first port of call was the vicarage and a quick final discussion with Sally about who had rsvp'd for the afternoon tea the following day. So far, Flora had heard neither hide nor hair of Edwina Edwards on the subject and she was secretly hoping the opinionated woman wouldn't turn up. It would be a village first if she didn't though, so Flora knew it wasn't at all likely.

The walk along Front Street was quiet, with Reggie playing his love-you-hate-you game with the fallen leaves and Flora herself deep in thought. It was only as they reached the village green and the duck pond, memories of Monday's debacle fresh in her mind, that Flora thought to call the parrot back to her.

It was too late, however, as Reggie was already hovering over the centre of the water, causing the few ducks to retreat to the banks as he screeched, "Cows loose! Here we go again!"

"What is it now, Reggie?" Flora asked, the exasperation clear in her tone. As far as she could see the surrounding area was empty – the opposite from earlier in the week – and she didn't have time to reenact the whole toupée scene for her parrot's enjoyment.

"Get out of it! All shook up!" the bird continued, dive

bombing the pond and pulling back just at the last moment so as not to wet his beak.

Flora was indeed beginning to feel all shook up. The lining of her dress was now sticking to her back uncomfortably as she stood at the end of the pond and peered across the water, looking for goodness knows what.

"Please God don't let it be another dead body," she whispered.

"Alright Flora?" The voice just behind her made her jump and Flora spun around to see James Marshall, complete with dog collar and bible under his arm, looking at her curiously.

"Ah yes, I mean no, um, tell me Vicar, can you see anything out there, in the middle of the water? Below where Reggie is making all that noise?"

James squinted and peered but had no more of an inkling than Flora. Reggie, though, was still in animated action above whatever had caught his attention and refused to come back, forcing the pair to conclude that the bird had indeed seen something interesting.

"Wait there, I've had an idea," James said, pulling his

mobile phone from his pocket.

And so it was that five long minutes later, when Reggie had done countless laps of the pond and Flora had made awkward small talk, that the new schoolteacher's husband – Chuck Fields, a burly, middle-aged American who looked like he could take on a whole boxing team single handed – arrived with his camera drone.

"I remembered Chuck telling me after the service a few Sundays ago about his latest toy," James said happily, "now, as much as I'm intrigued, I really must get on with my home visits."

So Flora was left, with a parrot who had his feathers in a fluffle and an outdoors survival expert who looked like he could eat her up for dinner.

"Right there," Chuck said, showing Flora the drone footage on his electronic tablet after flying the thing around for a few minutes, scaring the local wildlife and sending Reggie hurrying back to Flora's shoulder to hide in the nook of her neck, "something sure is bobbing in the water."

"A dead body?" Flora asked.

"Ah no, why would that be your first… anyway, no,

it's something long and thin I think. A bottle maybe?"

"Ooh, now that could be useful!" Flora clapped her hands in glee, aware that the newcomer must think she was as mad as a bat, "Well done, Reggie, my boy. All is forgiven!"

McArthur was as animated as Flora had ever seen her – which is to say her face was a tiny bit flushed and her mouth turned up ever so slightly at one corner – coordinating the retrieval of the newly discovered evidence. Unfortunately it was Timpson who had been called on to take one for the team, and as the bedraggled man waded his way back to them now Flora prayed that it wouldn't just be a vintage coke bottle that her wayward pet had suddenly taken a liking to.

Thankfully, it was indeed a glass wine bottle though the detective was saddened to discover the label had already peeled off and no doubt disintegrated.

"Stupid biodegradable rubbish," McArthur muttered under her breath, bagging the wet item the moment her soaked colleague passed it over.

"I think Sally will have some spare clothes in the

vicarage," Flora said kindly to the shivering young man.

"No… need… in car," he spoke through chattering teeth.

McArthur didn't give her retreating colleague a second glance as she turned the transparent bag in her hands over and over, "Well, it was floating because the killer was stupid enough to put the screw-on cap back on before throwing it into the pond," McArthur spoke to no one in particular, though Flora stood beside her listening with Reggie on her shoulder, eating one of the 'emergency grapes' that she kept in her handbag for calming the parrot in unexpected situations – of which, unfortunately, her little village seemed to have more than its fair share. "Can't identify it without the label though. I'll have to ask the shopkeeper again if she has any recollection at all of what kind of wine it was. Any memorable picture on the label, anything the deceased might have said about it. She says it was English in origin so there has to be a lead there somewhere, it wasn't your general supermarket staple brand. The bottle itself is innocuous enough, no specific defining features. Was it symbolic throwing the evidence where the man's hairpiece had been chucked, or just coincidence, maybe I'll…"

Flora walked away and left the detective to her monologue. It wasn't even ten in the morning and already there'd been drama. A cup of Earl Grey and a custard cream was needed, a good chat with the vicar's wife and then back to the tearoom for today's impromptu Knit and Natter group.

Flora had a feeling it was going to be a long old Friday.

THIRTEEN

It was Amy's day to work in the bookshop. A highlight of Flora's and her customers' week as little Barney always accompanied his mum and was the centre of attention, normally attracting quite a crowd. The toddler was almost one now and had such a cheeky smile and squishable cheeks that it was impossible not to fall in love with the mischief in his bright eyes. Of course, Reggie's beak was always put out of joint at not being the centre of attention, and he had long ago relegated the little lad to the status of " bad bird."

"Green isn't a good colour on you, Reginald," Tanya laughed at her own joke as she carried a large teapot full of Earl Grey through to the book nook, where Amy and Flora had just finished arranging ten chairs in a circle.

It had been Amy's idea to have an impromptu meeting of the Knit and Natter club – partly to ease the hurt of the Yarn Wars gig falling through for the older ladies, but mainly to encourage the group to help her fill a basket of goodies for Rosa who was bed ridden for the last part of her pregnancy. To show her she was in their thoughts. Flora had thought this a lovely idea and had mentioned it whenever it was appropriate throughout the week in the tearoom, asking for donations to be brought along this afternoon. Gifts didn't need to be bought, but weren't expected to be handmade either, all were welcome.

As the ladies started to filter in, with Betty and Hilda May at the helm, Flora was surprised to see Amanda Brookes among the group.

"I didn't realise you were still in the village," Flora smiled as she handed the visitor a china cup and saucer.

"Well, the recording for the show was meant to be done by yesterday, so that's when my train was originally booked for, but given the sad circumstances the detectives have asked us all to stay on until Sunday. I'm not sure why, really, I could do with getting back to my cats."

"Oh, are they okay while you're away?" Flora was an expert at feigning interest in small talk whilst also dishing out drinks and cakes.

"Yes, a neighbour has them. They're quite a handful, but they were my late mum's and I can't bear to give them up."

"Oh, I'm sorry for your loss," Flora said, watching Betty slap a huge scoop of clotted cream onto her fruit scone.

"Thank you," the woman whispered as the tinkling of a spoon against bone china caught everyone's attention.

"So, ah," Amy paused nervously and looked to Flora for reassurance. Once she'd been given the nod of approval she continued slowly, "So, I had the idea we could get together to make up a gift hamper for our Rosa. As you will have heard she's doing okay, the baby is fine, but the doctors need her to rest to keep her blood pressure steady and because of the position of the placenta causing some bleeding..." Seeing the looks on the faces of some of the older women, for whom such detailed information would have been kept private for propriety's sake in times gone by, she hurried quickly on, "Anyway, no cause for concern, I just thought we could show her how much she means to our little community." Amy took a deep, steadying breath and quickly sat down, lowering her eyes and focusing them on her son who played on a mat in the centre of the circle.

"Aye grand idea," Betty was the first to speak up, "of course I've already delivered two lots of handmade knits for the wee babby, so I've brought a packet of mints and a cotton handkerchief."

"Thank you Betty, that's um, very thoughtful," Amy nodded enthusiastically around for someone else to add their offering, as the door to the tearoom banged open and a gust of wind flew in, pushing a windswept Lily before it.

"Secrets and lies! Hide it all!" Reggie screeched from his perch, before just as quickly tucking his head back under his wing and going back to sleep.

"I'm so sorry I'm late," Lily hurried through and Amy gave up her own seat, opting to sit on the floor with Barney, "but Adam said I should come while he's up there at the farm to keep an eye on things."

"And we are so glad you did," Flora said, taking the two jars of raspberry jam and bottle of elderflower cordial that the farmer's wife thrust into her hands.

"For Rosa," Lily added, breathless, accepting a cup of tea from Tanya eagerly, "not had a chance to get in the farm shop much this past fortnight so that's my contribution."

"Perfect, thank you," Amy said.

"I was a bit limited on what I could buy without being allowed to leave the village, so the lovely Jean there suggested these from the shop," Amanda held up a bottle of bubble bath and some alcohol-free Buck's Fizz, "she was kind enough to invite me here this afternoon too."

"Lovely," Amy took them and added them to the wicker basket which Flora had brought from the manor house for this purpose.

Jean added a handmade pouch filled with lavender and a vanilla scented candle, Hilda May put in a beauty giftset of perfume and talcum powder that she had obviously been gifted circa 1990 and Flora contributed a selection of books, a crossword magazine and a beautiful pen she had bought while on holiday in London. Tanya's addition was a face cream and a small deer ornament which had been a present from her own mother in Ukraine.

It was when it was Shona's turn to add to the collection

of random items that the gasps began, as she brought out a beautiful satin nightrobe and gown. "For when she's feeling more like herself," the pub landlady said, blushing pink.

"That's gorgeous," Amy said, to sounds of agreement all around.

All apart from Betty, who could be heard muttering to Hilda, "I could have knit something better myself!"

Flora gave her friend a small glare, tempered with a smile as she said, "Well, that might've been a bit itchy," and the happy atmosphere prevailed. Baker's Rise had always looked after their own and this time was no different.

"I feel so bad that we can't put on an autumn fayre again this year. I know we'd all hoped it would be an annual event," Lily said, when the third round of cups had been filled and the scone plate was looking decidedly bare.

"Well, it wasn't really a success in the first place, so I wouldn't fuss yer head about it," Betty said, clearly on top form for a Friday afternoon.

"I think what Betty means, is that since the event was marred by murder, it perhaps isn't a village celebration we want to revisit," Jean said gently.

"Aye that's true, my Stan hasn't been right since," Lily's lower lip trembled and Betty patted her arm kindly.

"Don't you worry, lass, Baker's Rise will have him right in no time," the older woman had no real details on Stan's mental health issues, but her conviction in the abilities of community spirit was as stalwart as ever.

Shona shared her belief, "Yes, my Will is much better since everyone rallied round and got his vet appointments going again after he had that broken bone."

The women shared their stories of when Baker's Rise had opened its arms and its heart to their families to support them through challenging times and Flora's heart gladdened to hear them. It was as she watched Amanda Brookes slipping out of the room unnoticed that she wondered if their camaraderie had highlighted the woman's own loneliness – a feeling Flora could well remember from her life in the city.

Not everywhere is like Baker's Rise, and for once she was grateful for that.

FOURTEEN

Adam was out at the men's meeting, Naomi was video messaging her friends about some group event happening soon, and Flora had taken the opportunity to have a deep bubble bath, complete with green face mask and hair oil.

"You look like Shrek," her daughter had giggled as Flora passed her open bedroom door on the way downstairs, still wearing just a towel as she'd left the new skin oil that had arrived that day in the kitchen and now needed to trudge down to get it.

"Sexy beast! She's a keeper!" Reggie added, his head cocked in interest from where he sat on Naomi's bed.

Flora wondered for a moment if he thought she had developed green feathers like him and was chuckling to herself as she entered the kitchen. Her mirth was short-lived however, as one glance through the large back window, expecting to see the rose garden and back lawns in their autumn plumage, and Flora was confronted by a sight even scarier than her own visage.

A man, peering through the kitchen window, bold as brass and not even trying to conceal his face with a balaclava or anything. Not that that would've been better.

"Agh!" Flora screamed, alerting the pair upstairs who she could then hear charging down the staircase to rescue her.

"Agh!" The trespasser shouted back, clearly as disturbed by Flora's face as she was at finding him there.

"Stay here Mum, we'll get him," Naomi raced through the kitchen in her dalmatian onesie, Reggie flying above her head, and paused only briefly to unlock the back door.

"No, leave it to…" Flora began, but her daughter was already out the door and chasing the intruder down. She hurried after them in her pink, fluffy slippers, wishing her offspring – both of them – weren't quite so headstrong.

Shrieks of "Get out of it! Stupid jerk! The fool has arrived!" could be heard in combination with the high voice of the teenager. In the end, it was the bird who got the kill, so to speak, as he landed on the man's head, digging in with his talons and pecking at his scalp causing the intruder to fall to his knees as he tried to grab the determined parrot.

By then, Naomi and Flora had both caught up, the latter rather more out of breath than she'd like to admit. They had all reached the front of the house now, and Naomi had already started calling Adam on speed dial – *thank goodness for teenagers and having their devices permanently attached to their being,* Flora thought as she tried half-heartedly to encourage her feisty feathered friend off the man's head.

Her quick call with Adam finished, Naomi then turned her attention to the man who had now stood up and was being verbally assaulted by the bird who still had his head in a vice-like grip.

"I'm recording you," the teenager said, holding her phone up, "so don't be thinking you can get away now. We have evidence." Flora couldn't have been more proud of her resourceful daughter.

"I just, I ah, had heard about the gardens and wanted to see…" he began.

"Don't be giving me that rot," Flora had recovered from her shock and unexpected exertion, though she really wished she was wearing more than just a bath sheet, "nobody comes skulking around someone else's property at half seven in the evening in September in Northumberland without a very dubious reason. For one, it's blummin' cold, for two, there's nothing to see at this time of year, for three, I know for a fact this is the third property you've been found poking around uninvited. So tell me, Chris, and don't give me that location hunting rubbish, just what exactly are you doing in Baker's Rise?"

"I'm working with Yarn Wars, I, ah…"

"Secrets and Lies!" Reggie screeched, confident that Flora now had the situation in hand, he had risen from his stronghold position and proceeded to drop a stinky package on the man's head for good measure.

"Eugh, how did you train him to do that?" Chris asked, scrubbing his forehead with his sleeve.

"It comes naturally," Flora replied, somewhat sardonically, "but let's not change the subject. You haven't been working on Yarn Wars for long, have you? I would even hazard a guess that you took the role just so you'd have an excuse to be in the village. What are you? A journalist? Writing a true crimes book?"

"I think he's just some kind of pervert," Naomi declared, "a sick pervert peering through people's windows. Disgusting." And with that she ran off to greet Adam who had just pulled up on the driveway.

"What's this?" Adam said as he ran to where they stood, Naomi updating him as they came, "What the heck are you doing here, frightening my family?" He grabbed Chris and pinned one arm behind the man's back before manhandling him back along the side of the building and into the kitchen.

Reggie had little interest now that reinforcements had arrived, other than vociferously demanding his tasty reward.

"Could you get him some blueberries out of the fridge?" Flora asked her daughter, rubbing her temples where a tension headache had just popped up.

"Apple!" Reggie demanded, coming to land on the edge of the fruit bowl in the centre of the table and eying up the Cox's Pippins there. Flora nodded to Naomi that he could have it cut up into slices, really not caring about her bird's dietary demands in that moment.

"So, speak up," Adam said, shoving the man onto a chair at the table and hovering over him menacingly.

Flora rarely got to see this aggressive side of her husband, it having been dormant since he left the police force, and was almost shocked at the change in him.

"Speak," Adam repeated, even more forcefully this time. To Flora he said, in an altogether different tone, "Please could you use my phone, love, and call McArthur. She was still in the church hall after I left the vicarage just now."

"Will do," Flora said, only then remembering what she was wearing – or not as the case may be – and taking the phone with her upstairs to get dressed.

It turned out that Chris was neither a journalist nor a writer of any kind. In fact, he was just a very strange man who had a ghoulish fascination with murder scenes and couldn't resist the opportunity to come to the small village which had seen more than its fair share. He had hoped to visit every crime scene in

Baker's Rise, reliving the events as he had read about them in the press, from the perspective of the actual locations. Flora was horrified. Adam had given nothing away, but she could tell that her husband too was worried by this new development. The man had been arrested by McArthur and Timpson for trespassing, but Adam knew he would be released without formal charge as strictly speaking no harm had been done on any of the three occasions he had been discovered. Presumably, Chris had been around other places in the village too, during his extended stay, but just hadn't been caught.

"We can't have this," Flora said after the unexpected visitors had left, "I mean, he could just be the first of many, we need to do something."

"Aye love, I know, let me think on it a bit," her husband replied, his brows tightly drawn and his mouth turned down.

"Do you think he killed Evans so he could stay longer? Is he that unhinged?" Flora asked.

"Doubtful, though I know it would make a convenient resolution. After all, he could've just made an excuse to stay on a few days, or done so quietly hoping not to be seen. It does make me wonder at his alibi though. I'm thinking if he's been out gallivanting every night, getting his weird kicks from murder locations, then why did that assistant Kirsty agree to be his alibi? I'm thinking it's because she also needed one herself. I'll get McArthur onto that in the morning. Just one last thing, love?"

"Yes?"

"Is that green a permanent thing, or..?"

"Oh!" Flora had forgotten all about her face mask and hurried upstairs to remove it, her face hot with the thought that she had carried on conversations with both McArthur and Timpson without remembering she was as green faced as her parrot. No wonder Timpson had been giving her some strange looks!

Passing her daughter's door once more she was struck by a memory which had registered in the moment but had been overridden by necessity in the circumstances.

"Hey you two," Flora sat on Naomi's bed, beside Reggie who had apple peel stuck around the edges of his beak and looked decidedly fruit drunk with happiness, "I hope you're not too shaken. I'm really sorry about that, we promised you a safe place and..."

"Don't be silly!" The teenager responded, "My snaps are going wild, everyone at school wants the deets."

"Oh! Okay, I probably should've said to just keep it between us. Never mind though, what I really wanted to say was, I love you and thank you for calling me mum earlier. It wasn't something I expected but I must admit I'd hoped that one day…"

"I love you too, Mum," Naomi pulled Flora in for a squeezy hug which brought emotional tears to her eyes, "but that green really isn't your colour!"

FIFTEEN

The next morning, Flora left Genie and Naomi at The
Rise preparing for the afternoon tea which was to be
held later that day and accompanied Adam down to an
impromptu community meeting in The Bun In the
Oven, organised by Pat Hughes at her husband's
request. Apparently the pub had been chosen in favour
of the church or church hall as Shona had offered to
put on half price bacon butties and the local policeman
couldn't resist.

"I suppose the fact it's in the pub might encourage a
few more folk to come along," Flora said to Adam as
they walked past the tearoom which was closed for the
day for the afternoon's event.

"Aye well, it is very short notice but we need to take this seriously and everyone needs to do their bit," her husband replied gruffly. Flora knew he hadn't slept well, tossing and turning as he thought about not just their own intruder but the possibility of an influx of morbid sightseers into the village.

"Oh, you didn't have a chance to tell me how last night's get together went," Flora tried to take his mind off things.

"Very well actually, we all took a vote and Baker's Rise Just For Guys was born. All very democratic like, but I'm not sure about the rhyming name. Harry assured us all it was necessary to keep the parish council off our backs, but basically we're going to meet the last Friday in the month for food and entertainment in the vicarage."

"Ah that's perfect, we can let everyone who wasn't there last night know about it at the get together this afternoon," Flora pulled her scarf closer around her neck to ward off the chilly autumnal air, "hopefully Lily can join us later too, even if it means leaving Stan for a bit."

Adam nodded, still deep in his own thoughts.

If it's worrying him this much, with all he's seen over the years, it must be bad, Flora thought to herself, hoping the upcoming meeting would provide more reassurance.

Thankfully the local pub was packed. Most likely with villagers keen to hear what gossip-worthy event had prompted the meeting, but still, it meant that Adam could get his point across to as many neighbours as possible all in one go.

Pat Hughes looked distinctly uncomfortable with his role as organiser, public speaking not his thing at all, so he passed quickly over to Flora and Adam, grabbing another bacon bun as he walked past the bar as reward for his efforts. His police dog, Frank, who had so far lain peacefully at Tanya's feet, now whined and sniffed the air unsubtly until Pat gave him a share of the good stuff.

"So, ah, no need to panic..." Flora began.

"When they start with that, you know you should be panicking," Betty piped up, picking the bacon fat out of her sandwich, her nose scrunched up in disapproval, and feeding it to little Tina on her lap.

Flora gave her friend a stern look before continuing, "Now, you all know how many murders we have seen here in Baker's Rise over the past couple of years..." she went on to detail last night's events at The Rise and those earlier in the week in other murder 'hotspots,' keen to emphasise that the culprit had been apprehended, before finishing with, "and this village isn't a living museum to true crime. It's a homely, cosy place where we all know each other and look after each other. We need to work together to keep it that way."

"This might just be the tip of the iceberg, the first of many gruesome sightseers and social media stars who think they can get views from the macabre," Adam took the baton after Flora's call to action, his tone solemn, "and we can't just expect Pat Hughes here to be everywhere at once. We need to take responsibility for our properties, for our village ourselves and to that end I suggest we create a more formal Neighbourhood Watch group, taking turns to have a wander around, looking for anything or anyone suspicious. Individuals and families can contact the group headquarters at… it will be at The Rise, won't it Flora?"

Flora nodded though they hadn't discussed any of the logistics before the meeting began. She wondered briefly what housing a community headquarters would entail.

"Yes, up at the big house," Adam continued, "you can contact me or whoever is on the rota and we'll spring into action. Forewarned is forearmed," he concluded, rather ominously his wife thought.

"Ooh, we can call it Baker's Rise Neighbourhood Eyes," Hilda May said excitedly, looking to the two vicars for affirmation.

James Marshall and Christopher Cartwright shared a look which Flora could well interpret before agreeing to the suggestion.

"Sounds good, we can put it to the parish council," James said.

There was nothing the village liked better than a good social cause to bring them all together, in the style of 'us against the world' and much chattering now ensued around the tables. Adam laid out a sign-up sheet and Dr. Edwards was the first to put his name, "Now I'm, ah, retired I have a lot of time on my hands," he said loudly, and just to Adam, "and rather too much time at home with Edwina."

Adam nodded sagely and then passed the pen to Tanya who scrawled her initials, "I'm up for a fight," she declared proudly, and Pat beamed his approval from the bar, where he was 'just checking' how many bacon butties were left.

"In for a penny..." he muttered, helping himself to

another, as the dog beside him licked its lips.

Leaving her husband to do the admin, Flora spotted a hunched figure in the far corner, apparently totally oblivious to the meeting going on around him. She had no doubt that Grimes had just been drinking his sorrows away, without any intention to come to the community gathering. Certainly, none of the other Yarn Wars team were there.

"Mr. Grimes, I hear you can leave tomorrow," Flora took the spare seat next to him without asking, "that's good news, isn't it? I'm sure you'll be glad to see the back of Baker's Rise," *and we'll be glad to see the back of you,* she thought.

Two bloodshot eyes were briefly raised in her direction before focusing back on the half-drunk pint on the table.

"Grimes, are you okay?" Flora asked, thinking she should ask Shona to stop serving the man given it wasn't even lunchtime yet.

"I should've left after last season, or even better, as soon as they brought that clown on to present it," Grimes muttered, more to himself than to Flora. She cocked her ear, though, keen to catch any important detail that might crack the murder case.

"What happened last season?" Flora asked, when the man had fallen silent again, deep in his cups.

"You know, when Bruce made the call that old woman should be disqualified for dropping three stitches at once, even though she'd just sneezed."

"That's not the end of the world, is it?" Flora was curious.

"It is when the contestant in question goes back home and ends her own life on the night the show airs over the embarrassment she feels, then legal get involved, we have gagging orders on set and it's all so... ugly," he finished the last word on a huge hiccup and fell asleep laying across the small table.

Flora took the pint glass over to the bar, her head swimming with this new information. She would tell Adam, of course, on the way home, but how could it help the investiga...

"Is Dr. Edwards here?" The pub door flew open and a wild-eyed Laurie entered, scanning the room as Matias squirmed in his arms. Sally immediately rose from her seat near the door and took the small boy, sitting him on her lap.

"I am," Edwards spoke up.

"I know you aren't the village doctor any longer, but would you be prepared to…" Laurie was breathless, his face wet with either sweat or tears.

"Always, I'll always help a neighbour in need," Edwards said so that everyone could hear, as he followed the distraught man back out.

"That's our cue too," Betty said, rising more slowly from her seat and handing the terrier to Harry.

The ladies filed out after her, and Flora too. If Rosa and the baby were in trouble then they would all be there to support the small family.

Baker's Rise looks after its own.

SIXTEEN

One of the downsides of living in a rural area is the length of time it can take for an ambulance to reach you in an emergency. So, it was a tense twenty-five minutes as Rosa lay contracting, five weeks before her official due date, her waters having broken and not been as clear as they should've been. There was some worry about the placental position, which Flora didn't quite understand, but it was serious enough for the situation to be classed an emergency.

Doctor Edwards checked Rosa over, deemed there was nothing he could do but let nature take its course and then intervene if needed, and then waited in the small sitting room in case things should progress more quickly than everyone hoped and the baby want to be born before the paramedics could get there. Adam sat with him, and Laurie too, as the women had taken over in the bedroom and kitchen. The poor dad-to-be was understandably in a highly agitated state, and the doctor offered him a swig of strong stuff from a hip flask he kept in his coat pocket, explaining that there are some times tea just won't do.

It's a good job Betty didn't hear that slanderous remark, Adam thought, as he tried to distract Laurie with tales from his police days.

The women jumped into action, not even needing to voice the delegation of roles, just getting on with things in a demonstration of smooth efficiency. Tanya made hot drinks for everyone, Flora lit calming candles in the bedroom and filled a jug with iced water for the mother-to-be, Jean and Betty helped Rosa into a fresh nightgown whilst Hilda made swift work of changing the bedsheets like a pro. Sally had taken Matias back to the vicarage to play with her girls and so after the flurry of activity, peace reigned in that small bedroom. Laurie had the idea to get Rosa's mother in Spain on videocall and so she and Rosa chatted as the ladies sipped tea around her, standing tall like angels of light who would never give up their protective posts. Gabriela, Rosa's mum, was introduced to everyone virtually, and other than the contractions – which were getting closer together and more regular – it could have passed as a social gathering.

No one was visibly shaken nor panicked, but when the sirens could be heard entering the village at Baker's Bottom there was a collective sigh of relief. Just like with Amy last year, the women had come together to help one of their own in her vulnerable state and they shared smiles of satisfaction in a job well done.

With promises to let everyone know as soon as there was any news to share, Laurie joined his wife in the ambulance.

"Thank you for that," Flora said to Edwards as everyone left the small flat.

"Always here if needed, I know it's a long way to the health centre in Alnwick," Edwards said, for once lacking his usual pomposity, "I do regret my previous actions, Flora, very much. I know I've done some unforgivable things – indeed, I've had a lot of time to think on them, and Edwina reminds me daily that it's my fault we're ostracised in the village."

"Well, we hope to see you both up at the manor house this afternoon," Flora said, feeling the man's admission deserved her being magnanimous in return.

"Aye, that'll be grand, thank you Flora," the man said softly, and walked off in the direction of his own home, his steps holding a new humility.

"Well, that was a bit intense," Adam said as they walked home after collecting the sign-up sheet from the pub.

"It was, but we're experts at it now!" Flora said, still high on adrenaline.

"So, what time is everyone arriving?" Her husband's tone betrayed the fact he wasn't exactly looking forward to having a houseful later.

"Half past three, so we have… eek! Less than three hours! Best get a hurry on!"

Adam sighed, and Flora knew he was thinking about the televised rugby match he'd be missing.

"You did a great job back in the pub," Flora hoped some positive reinforcement would buck him up a bit, but in mentioning the morning's meeting it caused her to recall what Grimes had said.

She repeated it as close to verbatim as she could remember, adding the proviso that the man was drunk and so maybe not a credible witness, before saying, "That could be a motive for someone, couldn't it? If their loved one had been on the show and took their own life because of it? Because of Evans' decision."

"It could indeed, love, it could indeed. I'll get McArthur onto it as soon as we're back home. Many a truth is spoken from the mouths of the inebriated."

Flora squeezed her husband's arm where hers was linked with it, happy they always worked as a team.

Apparently teamwork was not making the dream work back up at the manor house, as Flora and Adam arrived home to find Reggie relegated to his naughty perch in the laundry room.

"He took the strawberry slices off the top of the Victoria sponge cake, one by one, when we were icing the mini carrot cakes," Naomi whispered, but Flora could tell she thought the parrot's antics hilarious, as her daughter could barely contain a giggle, "Aunt Genie was fuming! We didn't notice until there were only three left, so that's why his face feathers are stained red!"

"Oh my goodness, Reginald Parrot!" Flora shouted

from the hallway, and waited until she heard the familiar flap of wings.

"My Flora, love you," the bird cosied up to the nook of her neck and rubbed his still-wet face against her skin.

"Don't be thinking you can butter me up so easily," Flora said, "I hear you've been a bad bird."

Hearing the words which he knew to be a negative moniker, Reggie took to flight again, perching on the top of the function room door, "Bad Bird! Stupid old trout!"

"He called Aunt Genie that too," Naomi added.

"Well, I'd better go and apologise," Flora said, sighing heavily, "as if we don't all have enough to do."

Of course, Genie was absolutely gracious about the whole morning's shenanigans and had even managed to make an extra batch of mini eclairs.

"I'm not sure how so many of the others got eaten," Flora could feel herself blushing.

Genie smiled knowingly and put the kettle on, they both deserved a sit down and a cuppa before the afternoon's excitement began.

Little did they know, how exciting it would be.

SEVENTEEN

The afternoon had started so well, with the guests arriving on time, Sally – for whom the tea party was in honour – had given a moving speech about how grateful she was to all of her neighbours for supporting her through her cancer treatment, children played, a cheeky parrot preened and Flora felt confident that the event would go off without a hitch.

In true village fashion, everyone had brought homemade bakes, despite Flora having catered for a small army. Edwina had brought her famous Battenberg cake, Betty her miniature Victoria sponges, and the lovely new schoolteacher, Joy Fields, had provided an American Key Lime Pie.

"I can't wait to try it," Flora thanked her when the woman had come to the kitchen to help carry through the teapots.

"I'm not sure what's wrong with the traditional lemon meringue pie," Betty began, and Flora was about to interrupt when her friend continued with, "but it does look very tasty. I'll be having a slice and my Harry too."

"That's high praise indeed," Tanya whispered to Joy when Betty had left the room.

"I got that impression," Joy laughed good-naturedly, "my Chuck would eat a whole one in a single sitting if I'd let him. He comes back from these survival expeditions starving. Apparently you can live off foraged berries and the like but it doesn't fill you up, that's for sure!"

"My Pat would waste away if he didn't have his three solid meals a day," Tanya agreed, "though he does like a good walk in the countryside with Frank."

"Well, Chuck is starting up a rambling, hiking, survival skills type group. He was known as a bit of an outdoors expert back home and he's brought the flyers with him, so maybe Pat would like to take a look?"

The women were interrupted by the back door opening and Kirsty the Yarn Wars assistant popping her head round into the kitchen, "Hope we're not too late? Flora did say it was an open house type thing but the front doors are closed and there seem to be a lot of young people gathering round there."

"Of course," Genie opened the door fully for Kirsty and Amanda to enter and accepted the shop-bought pack of jam tarts they had brought.

"I'd better not let Betty see these," Genie whispered to Tanya as the two newcomers were shown through to the front room, "she'll chew their ears off and suggest a baking class."

Guests were spread throughout the large sitting room and the function room, where Flora and Adam had laid out some tables and chairs for the occasion. The next game of Hide and Seek could be heard beginning on the floor above them, with happy children's shouts and the sound of many little feet running across the ceiling.

"It's so lovely to hear them carefree, like children should be," Sally said as Flora took the seat next to her and poured herself a cup of Earl Grey, "I really worried at the time how my girls would be affected by my diagnosis and treatment. By James and I being at the hospital so much. Then there was the recovery where I had to keep asking them to be quiet and still... anyway, it seems no lasting harm was done."

"They all bring so much joy, Sally, they themselves are brimming with it. You're both doing a great job," Flora said, just then thinking that she hadn't seen her own Naomi for quite a while.

"Ah, Flora, you might want to come and see this," Adam appeared in the doorway looking none too happy and Flora's stomach sank.

He led the way out of the main doors and onto the gravelled front driveway, where an impromptu ticket booth seemed to have been set up without either of their knowledge. Standing behind it, happily taking payment was Naomi, giving out tickets and directing the groups of teenagers onto the front lawns, from where they could be seen taking pictures and making social media videos. Flora was horrified and marched across without even thinking twice.

"Naomi? What is all this?" she demanded.

"Hi Mum, oh, I just thought since we were having people round, and I'm actually quite popular with the kids at school now I have the murder house connection, they kept asking to come over too and I thought I could…"

"No, no, no," Flora tried not to shout, pausing to take a big breath and channelling her exasperation into wringing her hands, hoping none of the inside guests could see what was going on. Then she reminded herself that she didn't care what people thought, people in glass houses and all that, and moved her hands to rest on her hips. She didn't want to lose her temper though, there had clearly been some miscommunication between their daughter and herself, and Flora just wanted to get to the bottom of it.

"This is not at all appropriate," Adam said calmly, leaving the two of them to go and shoo the children off the grass, though not before taking the shoe box Naomi was collecting the money in so he could reimburse everyone.

"I know how much you want to fit in, what a great feeling it is to belong," Flora said gently when she saw her daughter was becoming upset as the kids were being turned away by Adam, "but this isn't the way. Giving into people's demands, peer pressure, it just gives a false sense of belonging. Do you really want your home associated with death?"

"No, not really, I love it here," Naomi whispered.

"Well then," Flora gave her a big hug, "I would love you to have some friends from school over for a proper sleepover, but without any ulterior motives of scoping out the place, hey?"

Naomi nodded against Flora's chest and Flora felt her own eyes welling up with tears. She knew how she herself had felt when she first moved to Baker's Rise, how lonely and ill equipped for village life, and she hadn't even been under the same kind of pressure as her daughter was at school.

"I'm sorry," Naomi whispered as Adam returned.

"All sorted," he said, "no need for tears, no real harm done. Let's go back inside and enjoy the party, shall we?"

They walked back across the driveway with Adam putting an arm around each of his girls' shoulders and hugging them close.

This parenting a teenager was some hard stuff, he acknowledged silently and knew Flora must be thinking the same thing.

"My No Me!" Reggie chirped as they returned to the function room, having obviously been looking for his friend, "Two peas in a pod!" That made the young girl smile and she wiped her eyes.

"Can I go and play with the Marshall girls and the others upstairs?" Naomi asked.

"Of course," Flora said, "there's a tray of juice boxes and fairy cakes in the kitchen you could please carry up."

"And one other thing," Adam whispered so that only the three of them could hear, "all forgotten, all forgiven, okay? We're a team and we sort things out together. No need to feel bad. Love you."

"Love you," their daughter replied, her eyes bright once again.

EIGHTEEN

Trying to chat to as many people as possible, as was the way of a good hostess, Flora next perched on the end of a sofa beside Jean, who was sharing the velvet couch with Kirsty and Amanda. Joy Fields had the armchair next to them and was explaining about Chuck's new outdoorsy group, though to be fair none of the three women looked very interested in what she was saying.

"Oh, and here's the man himself. Do you have one of those flyers for Jean please, honey?" Joy asked her husband, who was wearing one of those multi-purpose, khaki, utility gilets with all the pockets. He'd been wearing it the other day too. Flora couldn't imagine what he could fill so many little spaces with, that the man could possibly need on a daily basis in this little urbanised corner of Northumberland, nevertheless she smiled and accepted a shiny leaflet too.

"Oh!" Jean said, looking at the flyer, a perplexed scrunch to her forehead, "Is that a barn owl? Now where have I seen one of those recently. It's plucking something from my old woman memory…"

"Ouch!" Kirsty jumped up, hot coffee staining her blouse and jeans.

"Oh my goodness," Flora said, "quickly, let's get you upstairs and out of those wet things before the heat scalds your skin."

Amanda took the now empty china cup and saucer as the production assistant was rushed away by their hostess and placed it on the coffee table beside her whilst Jean sat there, unmoving, trying to catch her train of thought.

"Never mind, I'm sure it'll come back to me later," Jean said, accepting a choux bun from a plate that Genie was handing around.

"I wonder if there's any news about Rosa and that little

babby?" Betty spoke up from the sofa next to them as Flora returned to the room having found some spare clothes and checked that Kirsty wasn't burned. Apparently the poor woman had just got a shock and so was going to head back to the B&B in Witherham to finish her packing.

"I'm sure we'll hear as soon as they're ready," Jean said as Lily bustled into the room.

"Space for one more?" she asked.

"Always," Flora smiled as the farmer's wife took the space that Kirsty had vacated, luckily no coffee had reached the velvet fabric of the seat.

"Was that my Laurie and Rosa you were asking after?" Lily said as Tanya passed her a hot drink and Flora rose to fetch a plateful of cakes from the table under the bay window for their new guest.

"Aye, any news?" Betty asked, pieces of raspberry and white chocolate muffin spraying from her mouth as she spoke.

"Laurie phoned just before I left the farm to say the baby was born almost as soon as they reached the hospital, and that I'm to tell you she's a beautiful little girl, but as she's so early she just needs a small stay in the neonatal intensive care unit, just for jaundice and to take on some oxygen while her lungs wake up. Nothing serious though, considering she's five weeks early, Laurie says she's as healthy as could be. Six and a half pounds too! No name as yet, I just can't wait for a photo!"

Flora felt a flush of warmth in her chest at the news. Laurie and Rosa had asked her to be godmother and Adam godfather to the new arrival months ago, but she wasn't sure if it was common knowledge and so kept the joy she felt to herself. For sure, this would be one very cherished little girl.

"Aw, another bouncing babby for the village to love on," Betty said, "these bairns mek my soul happy, so they do." She smiled across at Amy who was trying to balance Barney on her knee whilst eating an éclair.

"Here you go, Betty," Amy said, smiling widely, "you can bounce this babby while his mum has a hot drink! Gareth's out on a plumbing job so I've got Lewis upstairs too."

"Of course," Betty grabbed the wriggling infant and held him close to her, immediately humming a nursery rhyme from her own childhood. The little boy stilled and listened, twirling a grey curl around his finger and watching the older lady's face intently.

"That's fantastic news, and calls for a celebration," Flora said to Lily, "I'll get Adam to bring some wine up from the basement. How's Stan doing?"

"A bit better, actually," Lily whispered back while the others were transfixed on Barney, "your Adam told him about the men's group and although it's still touch and go with never knowing how he's going to feel when he wakes up on a morning, he has been venturing out of the bedroom more these last couple of days, having a cuppa by the fire with Bertie and me. Said he might get back out to the barns next week too. I've told him to take baby steps, that there's no quick fix, and I'm there for him all the way."

"Aw that is good news," Flora said, "maybe he could reach out to the doctor when he's ready too."

"Aye, I asked him to come with me today, but he wasn't ready for a big group, you know. I think he'll chat more with Adam this next week, though, which is a huge step forward."

Flora smiled, relieved that Adam had been able to help in more ways than one up at the farm, only then tuning back in to the conversations going on around her.

Jean was chatting with Amanda about Evans' death, the latter having said how scary that must've been to wake up and find a dead body on your bed, especially having held the man in such affection as to have a room dedicated to him. Jean looked slightly astonished at that, but presumably assumed as Flora did in that moment that the woman had heard the grisly details in the local press.

"Aye, it wasn't the best moment of my life, I can tell ye," Jean said, "nasty business. And the thought of someone with those intentions being in my wee flat, well… to tell you the truth I've not been sleeping well."

"Oh no, you're welcome to stay up here anytime you like, Jean," Flora said kindly, having felt a similar fear every time she'd had a close shave with a killer. More times than she'd like to remember, to be honest. She wished she'd caught onto her friend's understandable fear sooner.

"Aye, I might take you up on that, Flora lass, I can't be having Pat or Will, Harry or whoever is handy checking the place is empty before I go up every night, can I?"

Flora hadn't realised that had been the case, and felt bad for her, "We'll work something out, Jean, just let me get today over with and we'll make sure you're feeling more secure one way or another."

The Scotswoman's eyes were filled with relief and gratitude as Flora excused herself to go and share pleasantries elsewhere, stopping in the study where the men had assembled – a sneaky laptop screen showing the rugby match having been hidden under a blanket just a second too late as she entered the room – to ask Adam to fetch some wine to toast the new baby's arrival.

"That'll be a fair few bottles for all this lot, even at a half glass each," Adam whispered as he joined his wife in the hallway.

"Well, some people won't have it and we don't need to use the good stuff," Flora replied, not particularly precious about her inherited wine collection anyway.

There was so much to be sad about in the world, it was worth celebrating the wins, Flora knew, and the afternoon's special delivery could've gone so differently for Laurie and Rosa.

"Right you are," Adam agreed, heading to the large room that ran under the building and grabbing Pat to help him carry the haul.

Flora took a moment to catch a breather in the kitchen, where the children had finally settled down and were sitting around the kitchen table. Naomi was in the process of painting the Marshall girls' nails and sported numerous bobbles and clips all over her head curtesy of the youngsters.

"Very fancy," Flora complimented her daughter on the look.

"It was me mainly, with a bit of help from Charlotte," little Evie said, looking proud as punch.

"And a grand job you've done too," Flora smiled and cut them all some apple pie. There was so much food they'd probably be eating it all week.

NINETEEN

With wine glasses collected from the cabinets in the function room and an assortment of wines to choose from, Flora suggested everyone get a drink in hand ready to toast the village's latest resident and her no doubt exhausted parents. Lily had even managed to get Laurie on video call and they all took turns waving to he and Rosa through the phone.

"Okay then, let's say cheers," Flora tried to hurry the group along, so as to leave the new parents in peace.

There was much bustling about, clinking glasses and wishing the family well, with Sally holding Matias up so he could wave to his mum and dad and the ladies fussing and cooing, asking for details. It was rather more than Flora had intended, with disturbing the couple in the hospital not part of her original plan. Not that it really mattered, as the pair seemed buoyed on adrenaline and relief, happy to share their joy with their neighbours and grateful to be able to show Matias that all was well after the fraught morning they'd had and before Laurie went back down to the NICU to visit their daughter.

"We've named her Gabriela Liliana, after Rosa's mama and my godmother, Lily," Laurie said happily.

"Oh wow, that's, that's, just lovely," Lily said, moved to tears as everyone clapped.

Such an emotional moment, that it was only after the call had ended and everyone sat back down that Flora noticed all was not well with one of her guests.

"Jean? Jean?" Flora shook her friend, who sat on the sofa alone, her head hanging forwards over her lap. "How long has she been like this?" Flora asked, getting desperate now.

The tone of her voice alerted Tanya, who hurried to find Dr. Edwards, whilst Edwina came straight over to help try to rouse the older woman.

"Do you remember when you last saw her alert?" Flora asked the doctor's wife as they patted Jean's wrists and leaned her back gently, her head lolling now to the side.

"Um, before the toast, when the wine was brought through, she mentioned that she'd remembered what it was she forgot earlier. Something about an owl on a flyer being the same as the image on a wine bottle in her flat? Then we all went to fill glasses. I can ask around if anyone else saw anything. It was that visitor sitting next to her, wasn't it? The one from the TV show? Not sure where she is now."

"Yes, Amanda," Flora replied, her mind whirring.

By now the doctor had taken over and confirmed that thankfully Jean did still have a strong pulse, but she was more than asleep. Likely sedated by the looks of it.

Flora grabbed the cups that were nearest Jean and asked Genie to take them to the laundry room and keep them separate from all the other used crockery as the remnants would need to be tested by the police.

"How can I help, love?" Adam asked, alerted to the situation when Tanya came to find Edwards.

"Can you do an internet search on English wines

which have an owl on the label please?" Flora said, and her husband did just that without questioning her reasoning.

"All shook up, here we go again," Reggie squawked, seeking Flora out as he'd picked up on the strange atmosphere – one that was unfortunately becoming all too familiar.

"Could you keep the children in the kitchen or the upstairs family room?" Flora asked Sally, as Dr. Edwards called for an ambulance.

"I can't rouse her, and best safe than sorry," he said by way of explanation to the women crowding round.

Genie brought a blanket from the basket in the corner of the room and laid it over their friend as Betty and Hilda watched on, horrified, and for once speechless.

"I've got it," Adam said, "vineyard on the outskirts of Winchester, why?"

"Amanda is from Winchester, she told me when we first met," Flora said and that was all that was needed to have her husband phoning his ex-colleagues.

"She won't get far," Adam said when he'd finished the brief call, "she's not got a car and taxis aren't exactly a regular feature round here. I bet McArthur will pick her up before she even reaches the B&B."

"But why would she do this to Jean now?" Flora asked as they moved away from the crowd and into the hallway, "I just don't understand."

"I think she's acted in haste, love," Adam said, "must've had some of the sedative left in her bag, probably wanted to give Jean just enough so that she felt ill and Amanda herself could offer to get her home. To get Jean out of here before she told us what she'd remembered about the wine label. I mean, to be stupid enough to gift drugged wine that came from her own locale… anyway, I think Jean's had a lucky escape, goodness knows what her fate would've been if Amanda hadn't mismeasured the drug and given so much that Jean can't even be roused. I guess that left Amanda no choice but to flee alone."

"Oh my word," Flora sat down heavily on a small chair in the hallway, "if she'd managed to take Jean out of here, she'd likely have…" she shuddered and rested her head on Adam's hip as he stood with his arm around her shoulders.

"Best not to think about it, sweetheart, but we should probably try moving everyone on. There's going to be quite a spectacle when the ambulance and the police get here."

So Flora roused herself into action, and began doing the rounds suggesting they all might want to start heading home. When most seemed to prefer the spectator sport that the sitting room was providing, especially since there was food left to be eaten, Flora announced loudly that anyone who stayed would be locked in and have to wait to give a witness statement to the police. Everyone knew how long that might take, so that got them up and out of there like rats up a drainpipe. With hurried thanks to their hosts and well wishes to Sally on her remission, the guests disappeared in groups until there was only the Edwards couple, Genie and Christopher, Flora and Adam left. Sally and James had taken their girls, Naomi and Matias back to the vicarage to keep prying little eyes and ears away from the worrisome scene in the manor house.

Tanya had offered to stay to clear up, as had the other ladies, but Flora had encouraged them to get home and cosy. Pat was off duty and there wasn't much the local policeman could do anyway under the circumstances.

To give her her due, Edwina had not moved from Jean's side, holding her hand and whispering words of reassurance that she hoped her neighbour might hear. Flora was grateful for her calm demeanour and said as much.

"We've been neighbours for thirty years," Edwina said, "I just want to see her okay again. It can't be healthy, being drugged twice in a week, can it Ernest?"

"Well, it's not good that's for sure," her husband replied, "especially at Jean's age, I would think it depends how much of the stuff is in her system."

"Should we try to get some water into her to dilute it or something?" Flora asked.

"Best leave it up to the paramedics," Dr. Edwards replied, "if Adam can tell them what was used in the original attack they might have an antidote or something."

"Good thinking," Flora said, as Genie entered the room with a tray full of hot cups of sweet tea for them all.

Now all they could do was wait.

TWENTY

The ambulance left with a still sedated Jean and Edwina accompanying her just as McArthur's car drove up the driveway to The Rise. The crisp afternoon had turned into a dank and drizzly evening and Flora shivered in her pretty tea dress as she stood with Adam waiting for his colleagues to reach them.

"Did you get her," Adam asked as soon as McArthur was within earshot, peering into the dark back seat of her sedan.

"Yes, as you suspected she was still waiting at the bus stop to get back to Witherham. Not the brightest criminal we've dealt with, obviously. I need to take quick statements from you two while Timpson waits with her and then I'll call back tomorrow with a full update. We'll be speaking to Jean Sykes again, when she's able, and that other woman who you said was there, Kirsty Bullmer.

As Adam gave McArthur the basic recap of events, she scribbling furiously in her notebook, Flora just couldn't help herself. She charged over to the car, opened the driver's door and slipped into McArthur's seat next to a shocked Timpson who simply opened and closed his mouth like a goldfish.

"Just tell me one thing, Amanda," Flora's voice was loud and urgent in the peace of the rural evening, as she swivelled to face the murderer, "why did you try to ingratiate yourself into village life? Befriending us, contributing to Rosa's basket of all things. You didn't need to as a cover up for your actions, you could've just slipped away, back down south without us even remembering your name. I'm sure the police would've caught up with you still, but why play with the friendship of the women in the village?"

"I guess I was just lonely," Amanda bit back, "you all have something I dearly want. That sense of camaraderie and community."

"And I'm sure you could've had that back home, if

you'd put yourself out there, and hadn't murdered or drugged anyone here!" Flora allowed herself to be helped from the car by Adam, who pulled her gently into his embrace and kissed her forehead as her body trembled from anger and shock. The week's events catching up with them all now.

"Come on love, let's get inside, you're freezing. McArthur will come back tomorrow to explain it all."

Flora let him lead her away, the sound of the car trundling back down the drive mixed with the rustle of leaves as the wind started to pick up.

"What a miserable end to the day," Flora whispered as she was met at the door by a small, green featherball, his plumage puffed out to ward against the chill night air.

"My Flora, so cosy, she's a keeper," Reggie chirped, hopping onto Flora's hand from where she snuggled him up to her chest.

"I know, Reggie, good bird," Flora whispered as Adam locked up behind them and hurried to put the kettle on.

"The tidying up can wait till tomorrow, love."

The next day dawned fresh and crisp once more, as if to draw a line over the murky proceedings of the previous afternoon and evening. Word had come from the hospital that Jean was awake and mostly well, but being kept in another night for observations, which was a huge relief to Flora as she sat in the kitchen at The Rise waiting for Adam to return from collecting Naomi from the vicarage.

It was her husband who entered the kitchen first, to say that Naomi had gone straight to her room, upset and shaken by recent events and her impromptu sleepover, which had apparently resulted in very little sleep due to the excitement of the Marshall girls and Matias crying for Rosa.

"I'll go up and speak to her," Flora said, removing her apron and taking her sweater from the back of the chair, "I've got a second dishwasher load on and have done a lot of the handwashing. Just leave the rest, Genie says she'll be over this afternoon to help me with it. I'm going to speak to her then about what we talked about before."

"Good plan," Adam said, "and you should have let me help you with all this, you look exhausted, love. I'll just get on with it now, then you and Genie will have time later to talk."

"I'll be okay, nothing a few days of rest can't fix," Flora said, having no idea when she would get those, "and thank you."

She kissed her husband sweetly and then set off to speak to their daughter who was being comforted by Reggie, the little bird's feathers damp with the girl's tears.

"Aw Naomi, it's okay, Jean is fine, the murd... culprit is in custody," Flora hugged the distraught teenager close and stroked her hair, "these feelings are normal. I've felt them myself many times, I guess I'm just getting more immune to the awful goings on now."

"I'm so sorry, Mum," the girl wailed, "I realise now it's not something to make a joke of or be proud of. I wish I hadn't let those kids from school come. Do you think my social worker will take me away?"

"What? No! I'd never let that happen, nor would your dad. We can even talk about making our relationship more permanent on a legal basis if you like. I called last night and told them you were staying at the vicarage, which was fine because Sally and James have had all the relevant checks through their church work. Everything has been cleared with the fostering team. They know the facts of what's happened this week and so they'll probably come to talk to you about it, but you will absolutely not be taken away. This is your forever home, if you want it."

"Yes," Naomi sniffed and Flora saw Reggie do something she'd never witnessed before. The little parrot clung to Naomi's knitted jumper with his talons, not touching her t-shirt underneath, so that he could spread his wings wide across her chest, his little face squashed into the girl.

It was the closest to a hug that the sweet bird could manage and Naomi and Flora laughed through their tears at the emotional sight.

"Ah Reggie, what would I have done without you these past two and a half years?" Flora whispered past the huge lump in her throat, "You really are the best bird."

For once the little parrot had no quick quip or salty retort, just a happy contented chirping, showing that he too knew he'd found his forever home.

TWENTY-ONE

It had been a long, emotional morning, with Flora and Adam ditching the cleaning in favour of snuggling in the family room with Naomi and Reggie and watching 'The Greatest Showman.' Adam had reinforced Flora's promise that the teenager was there to stay and they'd made plans to go to the theatre in Newcastle upon Tyne to see the pantomime that December, even buying the tickets right then to show that Naomi's first Christmas in the family was going to be a great one.

By the time Genie arrived and used her key to get in the back door, she found all three dozing on the sofa up there and a little parrot snoozing on the teenager's lap, so crept back down to do some polishing in the main rooms.

"Genie, you didn't need to do that, I was going to," Flora said around a yawn as she made her way downstairs an hour later.

"No bother at all, you know I like to keep busy. Thank you for getting the crockery sorted, we just need to get it back in the cupboards."

"Oh, that was as much Adam as me, a team effort, and he and I can put them all away later. For now, why don't we make a cuppa and have a chat, there's a couple of things I wanted to mention."

Genie looked rather concerned as they waited for the tea to brew and plated up some of the leftovers from the previous day.

"Are you enjoying living in the coach house?" Flora asked when they were sitting in the front room, her feet curled up under her and a blanket over her knees.

"Yes, very much," Genie said, her voice quivering.

"Oh!" Flora said, realising the woman probably thought she was about to ask for the little cottage back, "That's great, it's yours for as long as you want it."

"Phew," Genie managed a smile then and picked up her slice of banana and walnut loaf.

"Yes, of course, sorry I didn't mean to make you think otherwise. It was just a roundabout way of checking you aren't thinking of moving back into your family home. I've noticed it's still on the market."

"It is, and to be honest there hasn't been a single bite of interest. I'm not surprised really, since it's a dilapidated, old mausoleum that Christopher and I can't afford to have renovated before we sell. It's a millstone around my neck, to be honest, as now I'm paying for the upkeep costs since my sister's in prison."

"How is Vivienne?" Flora asked kindly, unsure whether Genie had kept in contact with her murderous sibling.

"She's not well, to be honest Flora, has been put in a psychiatric unit. I think she had a mental breakdown when mother died and just kept going downhill. Not that that excuses her actions in the slightest. Anyway, it was all a mess for a while, but when she was gone and I was able to gather all the documents from the house, Harry Bentley was so lovely and went through them with me. It turned out that my father's will – which I'd never seen, but I've told you how close he and I were, whilst my mother and Viv were always thick as thieves – well, it had a clause that said when my mother died then the house would become my sole property, anything in the bank accounts would be Viv's. Now, I don't know if Viv already knew this and she and mother had conspired to keep it from me, perhaps contributing to why my sister hates me so much but… well, all that to say, I have full ownership now which Harry has helped me to formalise, but I really just want to sell the place. Too many bad memories." She took a large gulp of tea and looked on the verge of tears.

"That's actually one of the things I wanted to talk to you about," Flora said, rubbing her friend's arm, "I've spoken to Harry too, not that he divulged any of the confidential information you just told me, just that he's also the accountant and solicitor for my holdings, and he agrees that the estate could buy the property, bring it into this century and then either let it or sell it. Obviously, only if you'd be happy to sell to me?"

"Oh my word! Oh my goodness, Flora you would be taking a weight off our shoulders, really. Are you sure it's what you want though? The place needs a heck of a lot of work."

"Absolutely, the estate hasn't invested in new property in the village since before my predecessor, Harold

Baker, who made a complete pig's ear of the accounts and nearly lost everything."

"Thank you, thank you so much, Christopher will be so relieved. He's seen how much it's been on my mind."

"Perfect, and you're very welcome. Just one more thing though. I know you and Christopher didn't get a honeymoon of any kind, and you're always working extra here, babysitting, birdsitting, making us meals, and Adam and I would like to return your generosity with a small holiday to Edinburgh."

"No! Oh my goodness," Genie was in floods of tears now and Flora gave her a hug, pleased to have lightened the load in her friend's life.

"You're not just my employee, Genie, you're one of the family, and we want you and Christopher to have a lovely break away, either now or in the springtime if you'd rather wait till it's warmer!"

"Thank you, Flora," and Genie's smile was all the thanks she needed.

"Was Genie happy?" Adam asked as the family of three sat around the kitchen table that evening eating a takeaway of fish and chips from the place in Witherham.

"Over the moon," Flora's smile was wide, "and it's made me think of other things the estate could do to lighten the load of the villagers in these challenging economic times."

"Oh?" Adam asked, but was interrupted by their daughter.

"Does this mean a raise in pocket money?" Naomi asked, a cheeky glint in her eye as she secretly fed tiny bits of her cod to the parrot on her knee.

"If there's an equal raise in chores completed," Adam replied, winking.

Naomi huffed, but Flora could see she was enjoying the exchange.

"Okay, I'll help with the laundry and ironing and clean my room once a week, is that enough?"

"Aye, if you're also keeping on top of your homework and cleaning out Reggie's cages regularly," Adam nodded and held out his hand, "it's a deal."

They shook on it and Flora and Adam clinked glasses, "Result!" Flora joked happily.

"Result!" Reggie parroted back, jumping onto the table where he knew he wasn't allowed and shaking his tail feathers.

TWENTY-TWO

The next morning Adam saw a very excited Naomi onto the school bus to Alnwick, the teenager clutching invitations for the Hallowe'en party Flora had said she could have up at The Rise.

"It's just six teenage girls, how stressful could it be?" Flora had said when she and her husband had discussed it the previous day.

Adam had simply raised an eyebrow and kept his thoughts on the matter to himself, wondering when his wife would stop adding so much to her plate.

It was a quiet morning in the tearoom, with the village

apparently still in slumber after the events of the previous week. It was Tanya's day off, Harry and Betty were driving to the hospital in Morpeth to collect Jean, whilst Adam was expecting an update from McArthur.

When the bell above the door rang at half past eleven that morning, it was indeed the two detectives, both looking as if they hadn't slept in days. Flora was once again glad that Adam had left that lifestyle and profession behind. It surely couldn't be good for their long-term health.

"You sexy beast!" Reggie landed on Timpson's shoulder, causing the young man to blush profusely. The detective had grown a beard recently, no doubt in an effort to appear older, and Reggie slid his beak through the wiry hairs as if knowing exactly how to wind the man up and embarrass him.

"Get down, you cheeky flirt," McArthur dismissed the parrot back to his perch to chants of "Bad bird!" and "Stupid jerk!" nodding reassuringly at her colleague. It was the first time Adam had seen any softening of the tension between the work partners and he was relieved they had finally begun to get along.

"So," McArthur began when strong coffees and shortbread had been served to all but Flora, who was having her favourite Earl Grey, "So, the suspect has been arrested. She confessed it all straight away, before we'd even reached the interview room, keen to get it off her chest I think. Not a bad woman as such, just a bit dim and very grief stricken. Her elderly mother had been a contestant on last year's Yarn Wars, had sneezed and dropped some stitches and the now deceased show presenter had disqualified her. Mother and daughter have different surnames due to a previous divorce, lived in different towns, so no immediate connection the production team could've made. Very sadly, the mother took her own life, so the suspect blamed the show and Evans in particular. The mother had been diabetic, hence the leftover needles and insulin, and the knowledge of it. Apparently Evans chose the suspect for the show, from the many competition entrants, due to her being some twenty years younger than the other applicants. If he hadn't been such a sleazy old goat and picked her, he might still be alive now. If she hadn't got the place as a contestant, maybe she wouldn't currently be locked up for murder. Chance is a strange thing."

Flora had struggled to keep up with the formal police language and McArthur's very fast monotone, so asked, "And Amanda was waiting in the back of the shop on the night of the murder?"

"She was," Timpson replied, "she also admitted to

deliberately bumping the arm of the other lady at the tea party on Saturday, so that she would spill her drink and cause a distraction when Mrs. Sykes was trying to recall the wine label."

"And she saw the shrine room when looking for the bed to put Evans on," Flora clarified.

"She did indeed," McArthur said, "none of those details had been made public, she could only have known about it from actually being there that night."

"But why did the production assistant lie about her alibi?" Adam asked.

"Apparently on the night of the murder, Kirsty Bullmer was staying over in Newcastle-upon-Tyne after a pre-arranged job interview at the BBC office there. Didn't want Grimes to hear of it if she wasn't offered the job. When creepy Chris asked her to be his alibi the next morning, it suited her to agree," Timpson explained.

"Well, that certainly ties all of that up," Adam shook his head, no hint of pleasure on his face, "this absolutely can't be allowed to happen again in this village. It's too much now. Well, it was too much with the very first murder of Harold Baker, but you know what I mean. Yes, I'm grateful that it led me to meet my gorgeous wife, but she and the villagers can't take any more murders in Baker's Rise."

"Aye, I know," McArthur said, her eyes full of compassion for once, "I've already put in a request to head office that Pat Hughes gets an extra bobby on the beat to support him. One man can't be everywhere between here and Witherham. The Chief Inspector is on board so it'll just be a matter of funds and timing. I really hope we aren't called back for another case on your doorstep as well, mate."

Seeing her husband so agitated and adamant that this must be the last murder in the village – although she agreed with him completely – gave Flora an unsettled feeling in her chest. The lid was threatening to come off her internal box where she placed all of the fear, the horror of the murder investigations she had unwittingly been part of.

"It's okay, love," Adam put his arm around her, sensing Flora's distress, "it's a lot, too much, for anyone to get their heads round. We lost Blackett, you lost Billy, the villagers have lost relatives and friends. This must be the last."

"Aye, Blackett was a huge loss. If it's within our power to make it so that there are no more killings here, then we will," McArthur promised and Flora fervently prayed that would be the case.

When the detectives had left, with assurances they'd keep in touch with Adam on a hopefully more social basis, Flora couldn't help but talk about the murders they had all been part of. The strange weapons of choice such as a frozen pie, a poisoned choux bun and a weighted Italian landmark. Adam listened quietly, glad Flora was getting it all off her chest, and stroking his wife's hair gently as the tears rolled down her face.

"No more living in fear," he promised when Flora could speak no more, so choked up was she on the emotions that had been set free by the detectives' visit. "I know I've mentioned this before, but if you'd like to see a therapist we can arrange that. If you need a break away after this latest tragedy, we can go back down to London and see a couple more shows with Naomi in half term. Whatever you need, love."

"Right now, just a bit of routine. Then I'll think about it," Flora said, stroking the soft feathers of the bird who'd flown across to console her.

"Right you are then, let's get back to some normality," Adam said, kissing her on the forehead and beginning to clear the table, "I could do with a bit of that myself."

TWENTY-THREE

Flora had never been one to do things by halves, and so threw herself into making it the best Hallowe'en party the girls had ever seen. It had been almost five weeks since the infamous afternoon tea up at The Rise, a time which had flown past as the last warmth of September had turned into a very chilly October, even bringing some frost in the mornings. Flora adjusted her witch's hat and admired the buffet of spooky treats – all created by herself this time – which included strawberries dipped in white chocolate with black chocolate chips as eyes to make ghosts, double chocolate cookies decorated as cat faces with green sweets as eyes and iced cupcakes made to look like zombie brains. Flora felt very proud of herself.

So far so good, as the teenagers had all been very polite, their eyes wide with awe as Naomi had shown them around the big house. Of course, Reggie was in his element, full of compliments and showing off as he insisted on joining the group for every activity. There had been a round of pin the tail on the Hallowe'en cat, a spooky memory game on a tray, and the traditional bobbing for apples which had been the parrot's favourite, given that he could wedge his beak into the fruit and keep it still for the girl trying to grab it from the water with her mouth. For a small price, of course, and only a minimum of three apple slices would engage his services!

Flora had predicted her pet's interest in the party games and so had created one where he could be the centre of attention, in the hopes that the little bird would then snore softly on his perch whilst the girls watched 'Hocus Pocus' on tele and drank fake witches' blood mocktails. This involved each of the girls trying to teach Reggie the phrase "Double, double, toil and trouble," since they were studying 'Macbeth' at school. They had one try each in the first round, and it would continue until the bird could repeat it correctly.

Well, it had seemed simple enough, until Reggie added his own slant on the entertainment by replacing some words with his own.

"Double cows loose!"

"Toil and jerk!"

"Corker trouble!"

Of course, the teens found this hilarious, and so Flora let it continue until Reggie realised he hadn't been rewarded for his efforts and flew into the kitchen in a huff. Placated with a slice of banana, Flora left the bird to his tenth snack of the day and gave out the confectionery prizes to all the human participants.

Adam had had the good sense to get out of hosting the event, as it was the first Baker's Rise Just for Guys full meeting at the vicarage, and he had gone early to collect Stan from the farm so they could go in together. Thinking she could do with some company herself, and keen to be more conscious of the potential loneliness of neighbours living alone, Flora had invited Jean, Hilda, and some other single ladies to pop in if they felt like a spooky treat and a cuppa.

In perfect timing for once, just as the girls settled down to watch the film upstairs, three pizzas and cheesy garlic sticks to share between them, there was a knock on the back door.

"Hello ladies!" Flora said, genuinely happy to see her friends, "Great timing as we've just finished all the games."

"Oh! We were hoping for a bit of Hallowe'en fun ourselves," Jean smiled as five women filed in behind her.

"In that case," Flora took them through to the function room, "would you like to be blindfolded and pin the tail on the black cat while I make the drinks?"

The older ladies giggled like schoolgirls over the activity, before praising Flora's ghoulish bakery skills. Compliments indeed for the woman who couldn't even work the oven at the tearoom properly when she first arrived and had taken baking lessons from anyone who would help her!

Of course, as soon as the food had been gobbled up, the girls upstairs became bored of the film and so began a multi-generational game of Hide and Seek, across all floors of the old building, and which lasted for over an hour. Naomi shocked her friends by hiding in the secret room in the study, so then had to show them the hidden passage from the laundry room to the function room too. The old place certainly provided a lot of places to hide, and by the end all were breathless and giggling, including Flora who had enjoyed just living in the moment for once.

Reggie hadn't quite got the hang of Hide and Seek, keen to know where his special people were at all times in case he really did lose them, and exposing their locations with squawks of "My Flora," and "My No Me." It all added to the fun, though, and Naomi declared it the best party she had ever been to, with her friends agreeing.

Flora wondered briefly how many parties the girl had had in her very unsettled childhood before deciding just to enjoy the pleasure that she had been able to bring her daughter on this occasion. She couldn't possibly hope to make up for all of the sad years the child had struggled through, but they could certainly make some great memories now.

"Yes, this is the best night I've had in years too," Hilda exclaimed, and Flora dared not mention the Italian night where the woman had seemed to enjoy herself rather too much earlier that year. She shared a knowing glance and a smile with Jean instead, who was currently having her nails painted purple by one of Naomi's friends.

"Wait till I tell Betty what she's missed," Jean said, her cheeks flushed, "that'll teach her to stay at home preparing her Christmas cakes."

"Well, I'm sure there'll be other times," Flora said, handing round cold glasses of bright green limeade, dressed with red glacé cherries to go with the theme, "I've thoroughly enjoyed partying with you all."

Long after the older ladies had gone home to their beds, and Adam had returned from a successful evening at the vicarage watching the latest Indiana Jones film whilst enjoying a curry, Flora could hear the girls whispering and giggling well into the night. They had opted to have a communal sleepover in the function room, with an over-excited Reggie too, and Flora could hear their happy voices drifting up the stairs until the early hours.

And she didn't mind a bit.

This was what she'd hoped for in those years of emotional drought with her ex-husband. This was what she'd dreamed about as she commuted long hours into the city each day in a job that had never fulfilled her. This was what she'd prayed for.

A family of her own.

And that was exactly what she'd been given.

TWENTY-FOUR

The church was fuller than usual that Sunday morning as Flora had mentioned to a few neighbours in the tearoom that week that she'd be sharing something important at the weekly service. Of course, in typical village style, the whispered news had snowballed from one gossip-filled chat to the next, and by the time Sunday morning came Flora was apparently going to announce the creation of a new leisure park on the lawns of The Rise, complete with spa and Olympic sized swimming pool.

So it was that Flora wondered, as she sat with Adam and Naomi in the second pew back from the front, whether her actual news might come as a bit of an anti-climax.

Before it was her turn to get up and speak, however, Flora listened to all of the usual end of service notices and then as Reverend James spoke about Sally's new venture.

"This will not be gender-based, crafting-skill based, nor for any level of musical talent and certainly not just for those who can afford it," the vicar stipulated, "this is a group for anyone in our community who fancies a chat over a hot meal in the church hall. The second Tuesday of every month, Sally will be hosting Baker's Rise Time to Socialise. Off the back of our excellent men's gathering just the other night, I know this will be popular, and there will be no limit on numbers, just sign up on the sheet at the back please."

There were whispers of approval and a general hubbub of chatter until James said that Flora had something to share, and the place was suddenly completely silent, the atmosphere thick with expectation.

"Hello everyone," Flora said into the microphone, suddenly full of nerves, "I hope I'm not about to disappoint any keen swimmers, as there won't in fact be a new leisure facility up at The Rise." There were a few titters of laughter and then silence once again. "What I did want to say, though, and to everyone at once so you all know at the same time, is that Adam and I have been discussing the current economic climate quite a lot recently, with Harry too and as always I'm grateful for his sensible advice," she paused to wipe a stray hair from her sweating forehead, "so, conscious of the fact everyone is stretched thin at the moment, we have decided to pause rent payments for any estate property for the next four months, taking us up to the springtime. A chance to enjoy the festive season with families and not worry so much about money."

Unusually for a church service, there was an actual round of applause then, with Lily suddenly bursting into tears, and Flora herself welling up as she saw the relief on the faces of her neighbours.

Nevertheless, she waited for the chatter to calm before continuing, "My predecessor, Harold Baker, had the view that the village was there at his personal disposal to be milked like some indebted cash cow. I hope you know by now that I do not share that view – I fervently oppose it in fact. The estate and the village are a symbiotic team, one cannot go on without the other. On a personal level, as we've all realised more in recent months, we need to support each other as things in the country at large put more and more pressure on small villages like ours. We need to stick together and give back where we can."

It was a carefully planned speech, but even though she knew the words off by heart, the effect they had on her neighbours humbled Flora even more and she was taken aback and somewhat embarrassed by the number of people who came to personally thank her and Adam afterwards.

"What with both the farm rent and that for the farm shop in the village, this rent holiday will give us a chance to get our heads back above water," Lily hugged Flora tightly at the end of the service, "thank you so much."

"This will make such a difference to Rosa being able to spend time with the baby and maybe just open the shop for half the week for the next few months, give her a chance to work out how to juggle things," Laurie said, his eyes glassy.

Flora swallowed down her emotion and nodded. If she'd known what a difference this would make, she would hopefully have thought of it sooner.

Better late than never, though, she thought to herself, *especially with Christmas on the horizon.*

If there was anything that could bring Flora back to beautiful normality quickly, it was a down to earth, everyone-pitch-in, no airs and graces Sunday roast dinner at Betty and Harry's. The open fire was lit, the potatoes mashed to within an inch of their lives, the Yorkshire puddings towering over everyone's plates and the gravy beautifully lump free.

"That was another gastronomical delight, thank you Betty," Adam declared, rubbing his full stomach and earning him an extra portion of apple crumble and custard.

"Now," the older woman said to Naomi who was helping her clear up afterwards, "I have something for you, my little star baker."

"Ooh! What is it Granny Betty?" The teenager asked, following Betty back into the kitchen eagerly.

"Well lass, being as how you're my adoptive granddaughter, I thought you should be in on the secret family Christmas cake recipe. Now, Granny Lafferty's original is rather too boozy for a young'un like you, so I've baked you your own small version. You'll need to take it home and feed it regularly with fruit tea – I'll show you how – and then when it's time you can bring it back down here and I'll teach you how to ice it."

Flora had fond memories of Betty doing that very thing with her two years ago, though with the strong stuff, "Actually, speaking of adoptive children, now is probably a good time to let you know that, after discussing it with our Naomi, Adam and I are submitting the papers to adopt her properly."

It had just blurted out, they hadn't planned to announce anything until it was all finalised, but the intense delight it gave Betty and Harry made Flora glad of her slip up.

"Aw that's grand lass, best news ever," Betty squeezed Naomi and then Flora, opting to pat Adam on the head affectionately, "well if we're sharing secrets, I can tell you that I got your granddad Harry here to order you some figurines for the top of your cake from that musical, 'Frozen,' that all the bairns seem to love. I haven't seen it myself, but the Marshall girls have all the toys."

Flora cast a nervous glance at Naomi, hoping she wouldn't mention that the film had been aimed at five year-olds. She needn't have worried.

"Oh, that's so thoughtful, Granny Betty, thank you.

They have the live version of the musical on in London and I'm thinking of asking for tickets as my Christmas present from Mum and Dad. I can't wait to ice the cake with you."

It wasn't just the log fire which warmed Flora right down to the tips of her toes, and for the second time that day she had to swallow down a rush of emotion, so grateful for their extended, adopted family.

TWENTY-FIVE

That Tuesday afternoon saw another first, as the village ladies gathered in the book nook for the inaugural meeting of what Flora had called, 'Wool Warriors.'

"Now, that whole thing with Yarn Wars last month got me thinking," Flora began, when everyone had been adequately fed and watered, and Reggie subdued with a fat grape, "that instead of competing with one another, we should be collaborating."

"Just what I always say," Betty nodded whilst feeding the last crumbs of her second scone to Tina on her lap.

Everyone smiled, all thinking the same thing, and Flora

continued quickly, "So, I thought our first project could be a collectively created blanket. We would each knit or crochet, however you want, a three by three square contribution – that's nine granny squares in total, I may still need some help with mine…"

"And me," Tanya interjected.

"Then we could sew them all together and auction the blanket off at Baker's Rise Stars In Their Eyes next month." Flora continued, "I'm not sure if you know this, but a huge percentage of foster children in this country move from home to home with their few belongings shoved in a black plastic bin bag. It hardly affords them any sense of worth or dignity. If you all agree, I'd like to use the money raised to buy from a charity who makes proper backpacks for these children to use, then we could give them to Children's Services at Northumberland Council to distribute."

There was a unanimous sound of approval, with suggestions from the women of other things they could make to auction too.

"Excellent, then let's get started," Flora said.

"Actually, just before we do," Rosa spoke up softly, little Gabbi in the carry cot beside her having already been the centre of the group's attention for the first half of the gathering, "I know that you were sad, Jean, to lose your lucky knitting needles, and my mama in Spain wanted to thank everyone for their help when I was in labour, so she's sent a selection of needles, crochet hooks, delicate yarns and threads. Please just help yourselves."

There was a polite pause for all of a millisecond before the women descended on the wicker basket that Laurie had carried in for his wife when she first arrived. Rosa had repurposed the hamper that they had gifted to her and filled it with all the presents her mother had sent over.

"That is extremely generous, thank you," Flora said, holding back while the very unladylike scuffle continued between them.

"Not at all, we give where we can," Rosa said, "all appreciating each other."

And so the circle of village life continued, the pattern only varying occasionally when there was an event which bound them all together even more tightly for a short time, the threads of their tight knit community woven over years of shared struggles and celebrated triumphs.

"Is that your vintage typewriter I spot on the counter?" Jean asked Flora when everyone had calmed down again.

"It is," Flora replied, feeling the heat rise up her neck, "I thought I might write some books about a cosy community and the lives of the people there. A real feel-good, heartwarming story."

"I'd read that," Tanya spoke up.

"Me too," Hilda replied.

"Me too!" Reggie agreed, and they all laughed.

Thank you so much for your regular visits to Baker's Rise. The village needs a break from the murders that have plagued it, and so this is the last we'll see of our favourite characters for a while.

Not to worry, though, Reggie and an older Naomi will return soon in a new series, where we're sure to see some familiar faces from time to time!

R. A. Hutchins

*A cosy new series is now available featuring Reverend Daisy Bloom and her rather secretive neighbours. The **full trilogy is available** on Amazon worldwide, always free to read on Kindle Unlimited.*

*"**Fresh as a Daisy,**" is the first instalment in the **Lillymouth Mysteries** series set in North Yorkshire.*

Read on for an excerpt…

R. A. Hutchins

AN EXCERPT FROM *FRESH AS A DAISY – THE LILLYMOUTH MYSTERIES BOOK ONE*

Daisy Bloom hummed along to the Abba song on Smooth radio, pondering how she might use the lyric 'knowing me, knowing you' this coming Sunday, in the first sermon she would deliver in her new parish. She was barely concentrating on her driving in fact, knowing the roads like the back of her hand as she did. Barely anything changed around here, in this small coastal corner of Yorkshire, and Daisy really wasn't sure if that was a good thing or not. It had been fifteen years since she had left the town of Lillymouth, at the tender age of eighteen, and the newly ordained vicar had not been back since. Indeed, had the Bishop himself not personally decreed this was the parish for her – in some misguided attempt to help her chase away the demons of her past, Daisy presumed – then she suspected that she would not have come back now either.

Positives, think about the positives, Daisy told herself, pushing a finger between her dog collar and her neck to let a bit of air in. The weather was remarkably lovely for early July in the North of England, and Daisy was regretting wearing the item which designated her as a member of the clergy. She had wanted to arrive at her new vicarage with no possibility that they not immediately recognise her as the new incumbent – after that awful time when she turned up as the curate of her last parish, and they had mistaken her as the new church organist. Not helped by the fact that she was tone deaf... She knew she looked very different from the fresh-faced girl who had left town under a black cloud though, so there was a good chance even the older townsfolk wouldn't recognise her.

Anyway, positive thoughts, positive thoughts, Daisy allowed her mind to wander to the shining light, the beacon of hope for her return to this little town – her new goddaughter and namesake, Daisy Mae, daughter of her best friend from high school, Bea. Pulling up outside of the bookshop which her friend owned, and glad to have found a disabled parking spot so close, Daisy was surprised to find she was relieved that the old Victorian building had not changed since she left all those years ago. It still stood tall and proud on the bottom corner of Cobble Wynd and Front Street, it's wooden façade hinting at its age. The building had been a bookshop since Edwardian times, Daisy knew, and she smiled as she saw the window display was filled with baby books and toys – old and new coming together in harmony, something that, according to the Bishop, was far from happening in the town as a whole.

"Daisy!" the familiar voice brought a sudden lump to her throat as Daisy made her way into the relative dimness of the shop, the smell of books and coffee a welcome comfort. The voice of the woman who had been her childhood friend, who had been one of the few to support her when the worst happened all those years ago… *positive thoughts…*

"Bea," Daisy leant her walking stick against the old wooden counter and reached out to hug her friend, careful that her own ample bosom didn't squash the little baby that was held in a carrier at her mother's chest. Wanting to say more, but finding herself unable to speak around her emotion, Daisy tried to put all of the love and affection she could into that physical touch.

"Meet Daisy Mae," Bea said proudly, pulling back and turning sideways so that Daisy could see the baby's face.

"The photos didn't do her justice, Bea, really, she's beautiful." Okay, now the feelings had gone to her eyes, and Daisy tried to wipe them discreetly with the back of her hand. She wasn't this person, who was so easily moved – or at least she hadn't been since she ran and left Lillymouth behind. Daisy had funded herself through training and then worked as a police support officer for victims of violence for almost a decade, before hearing the calling to serve a higher purpose. She had survived assault and injury as part of her previous profession, seen some truly horrible things, and yet had not felt as emotional as she did now. Not since the day she quit this place, in fact…

"Aw, you must be tired from the drive," Bea, tactful and sensitive as always, gave her the perfect 'out', "come and have a cuppa and a sandwich in the tea nook. Andrew just finished refurbishing it for me."

"Thank you, but let me get it for you, are you even meant to be working so soon after the birth?"

"I'm just covering lunchtimes while my maternity

cover nips out for a quick bite – well, I think she's actually meeting her boyfriend, she never manages to stick to just the one hour, but, ah, she's young and well read… why don't you hold little Daisy while I get us sorted with something?"

"Oh! I… well, I…"

"You'll be fine, Daisy, you're going to have a lot of babies to hold during christenings, you know! I can't wait for you to christen this little one," Bea chuckled and unfastened the baby pouch, handing the now squirming bundle to the vicar without hesitation once Daisy had lowered herself into a squashy leather armchair.

Wide, deep blue eyes, the colour of the swell in Lillywater Bay on a stormy day looked up at Daisy with surprise and she found herself saying a quick prayer that the baby wouldn't start to scream. Daisy desperately wanted to be a part of this little girl's life, feeling as she did that she might never have a child of her own. What she had seen in her previous profession had put Daisy off relationships for life. As part of the Church of England she was not forbidden from getting married and starting a family – quite the opposite – but Daisy's own feelings on the matter ran deep and dark.

"Here we go," Bea returned with a tray holding a pot of tea, two china mugs, a plate of sandwiches and some cakes, "you look like you could do with this."

"You aren't wrong there," Daisy felt suddenly and surprisingly bereft as baby Daisy Mae was lifted gently from her arms and placed in a pram in the corner next to them.

"Have you visited the vicarage yet? Nora will be on tenterhooks waiting for you, she'll have Arthur fixing and cleaning everything, poor man!"

"I haven't had that pleasure," Daisy smiled ruefully, "I thought I'd come to visit my two favourites first," Daisy smiled back, knowing she was being slightly cowardly, but Nora Clumping was not a woman to become reacquainted with on an empty stomach. She had been the housekeeper at the vicarage for as long as Daisy could remember, surviving numerous clergy, and she had seemed ancient to Daisy as a girl. She could only imagine how old the woman must be now. She must have a soft side though, Daisy had thought to herself on the journey from Leeds, otherwise she wouldn't have taken Arthur in decades ago and adopted him as her own. Not that that diminished from the woman's formidable presence, however... for someone so slight in stature, she was certainly a powerhouse to contend with!

"Ah, wise choice," Bea agreed, "and if I were you, I'd pick up some fruit scones from Barnes the Baker's before you head up there!"

"Sound advice," Daisy laughed out loud, before remembering the baby who had now fallen back asleep, and lowered her voice to a whisper to joke, "I may be in the church now, but I'm not above the odd bit of bribery where necessary!"

"Just wait till you hear her views on the previous vicar," Bea said, not a small amount of excitement in her voice, "oh how I wish I could be a fly on the wall!"

"Argh," Daisy groaned exaggeratedly into her coffee mug causing her friend to snort.

"I want all the details afterwards," Bea continued, "I'll bet you five pounds that within ten minutes she mentions that time she caught you making a daisy chain with flowers you'd pulled from the vicarage garden."

"I was eight!" Daisy replied in mock protest, even while still knowing her friend was right – nothing was ever forgotten in small towns like these.

"Well, I've still got your back like I did then," Bea said,

reaching over to rub Daisy's shoulder conspiratorially, and adding with a wink, "and I'm sure she isn't allowed to give the new vicar chores as punishment!"

Perhaps coming back to this place after so long won't be so bad after all, Daisy thought. *With good friends like this, I can serve the parish, find the justice I seek for Gran and be out of here before the Bishop can say 'Amen.'*

The Bible says 'seek ye first the Kingdom of God' – well, I've done that, now I can seek out a cold hearted killer. They may have gotten away with it for over a decade, but divine retribution is about to be served.

Fresh as a Daisy

The Lillymouth Mysteries Book One

Whole Trilogy Out Now!

A new mystery series from R. A. Hutchins, author of the popular Baker's Rise Mysteries, combines the charm of a Yorkshire seaside town with the many secrets held by its inhabitants to produce a delightful, cosy page-turner.

When Reverend Daisy Bloom is appointed to the parish of Lillymouth she is far from happy with the decision. Arriving to find a dead body in the church grounds, leaves her even less so.

Reacquainting herself with the painful memories of her childhood home whilst trying to make a fresh start, Daisy leans on old friends and new companions. Playing the part of amateur sleuth was never in her plan, but needs must if she is to ever focus on her own agenda.

Are her new neighbours all as they seem, or are they harbouring secrets which may be their own undoing? Worse still, will they also lead to Daisy's demise?

A tale of homecoming and homicide, of suspense and secrets, this is the first book in the Lillymouth Mysteries Series.

*A brand new, **cosy romance series** for 2024 is coming in January!*

Take a stroll down Oak Tree Lane, the home of cosy community and healing hearts.

*Read on for a bonus excerpt from the first book in the series, **"Chasing Dreams on Oak Tree Lane."***

An Excerpt from *Chasing Dreams on Oak Tree Lane.*

This was not the way it was meant to begin.

They should have been here together, cleaning the place and deciding where to put everything, full of the excitement of starting a new chapter.

As it was, Meg stood alone and, she had to admit, rather forlorn on the main street of the little town she had chosen as her new home, water dripping from the sponge in her hand as she took a moment to catch her breath and take in her new surroundings. Washing windows this filthy was hard work. Not for the first time since she had arrived four days ago, Meg questioned her life choices. What had once been a shared dream had, when it actually became within reach, swiftly become a sole desire and yet Meg had stubbornly held onto it, ploughing ahead with their plans in the hope that he would change his mind. She had arranged the finances herself, offering the bank her inheritance and savings as downpayment to get a mortgage on the old place, convincing herself he could pay her half back when he came around to the idea.

The idea they had talked about for the past six years.

The idea they had made several trips to Lower and Upper Oakley to dream about and flesh out in the hope of catching a property before it was put up for sale to the public.

The idea that he then refused to even discuss.

The further Meg went with the project the further apart they grew, until the point of no return – moving day. Her notice period worked, her boxes packed, the frames and canvases out of storage and snuggly cocooned in bubble wrap, the van scheduled to arrive at any minute, and yet not a single item of his had been moved from its usual place in their shared flat. Then and only then did it really sink in.

She was doing this alone.

Again not for the first time since arriving, Meg wiped a stray tear from her cheek and straightened her protesting back, taking in her surroundings.

What Lower Oakley lacked in size it made up for in charm and location. Perfectly situated at the bottom of Oak Hill, the town was bordered on one side by beautiful fields which rose in a sharp incline to Cheen Castle and the twin town of Upper Oakley, and at the bottom by the North sea, where a small harbour protected a tiny fleet of fishing boats. Lower Oakley had only one main shopping street, Oak Tree Lane, from which all of the residential roads branched off. The whole area was named after the giant, centuries-old oak which stood proudly halfway between its two namesakes. Meg had visited this area often as a girl on holiday with her aunt and had developed what could only be described as a strong affection for the mighty tree, reading into it all kinds of life lessons, such as resilience and endurance. More than that though, the whole place made her heart happy, hence the fact she had just signed away her life savings to buy this prime, if somewhat dilapidated, spot on Oak Tree Lane.

The previous occupants had reluctantly left the place to move in with their daughter down south. Well into their eighties, the Scotts had been running their hardware store in the town for over half a century and were well loved by their neighbours. That the shop front had long since fallen into disrepair, and the irony that the inside hadn't seen a lick of paint for years despite the many tins of the product which the couple themselves sold, had all been overlooked by the locals, who always stood by their own. On the one hand, Meg was grateful that the place needed a thorough update, else she wouldn't have been able to afford it on her own, but on the other the sheer amount of work which now awaited her was thoroughly overwhelming – hence the window cleaning. Baby steps.

Brought out of her thoughts by a shrill shriek behind her and an immediate and rather harrowing wailing, Meg spun around to find a small girl on her knees on the pavement, the water from Meg's now overturned bucket spilling out around her.

"Billy's dead!" The child shrieked, causing not a small amount of alarm to swell in Meg's chest. How long had she tuned out for? And who on earth was Billy?

"I, ah, shall I help you up?" Meg bent down beside the chubby infant, realising from this closer vantage point that the little girl must be no more than four or so, judging by the ages of the children who had come to her after-school art club in Durham. That was the extent of Meg's knowledge of children, however, and when the child's wailing increased with her words rather than subduing to a less ear-splitting level, Meg had to admit she was at a loss. Her own knees were wet now as she ineffectually rubbed the tiny girl's back.

"Leave her, I'll see to her," it was more a growl than a clear command, but it had the effect of sending Meg jumping to her feet and several steps backward. Shielding her eyes from the midday sun, she squinted up at a behemoth of a man, complete with bushy beard and unruly blonde curls. The stranger himself sent a piercing glare Meg's way as he lowered himself onto his haunches, well above the puddle, and lifted the little girl into his arms before balancing her on a thick thigh.

"There, there sweetheart, it's just a bucket and some water, no need to be upset." As if the words were a magical incantation, the child's cries slowed, her face buried in the man's broad chest as he rubbed soothing circles onto her back.

Meg didn't know where to put herself of what to say. She felt like the outsider that she was and so hopped from one foot to the other, wringing her hands. If she was honest, she could really do with someone to rub soothing circles onto her own back, especially someone with big hands like that...

As if just remembering the unfortunate Billy, the infant jerked her head back to look at the man cradling her and through a series of hiccups and sniffles she whispered, "Daddy, Billy's dead."

"No he's not honey, he's just wet," the man soothed, pointing to a drowned-looking bear that was half hidden by the bucket which had clearly fallen on top of the toy.

"Oh, let me get that," Meg jumped to action, happy to have a job to occupy her, "I'm so sorry about the bucket, I..."

"Well you ought to be," the man bit back, standing to tower above her now with the little girl in his arms, his forehead bunched into frown lines, "leaving obstacles in the street like that."

Meg was about to retort with a strong argument in her defence, mainly focusing on the fact that it was a public path and where else was she to put her bucket when she was washing the front windows of the shop, when she noticed that trickles of blood were running down the little girl's legs below the hem of her flowery sundress. Following her gaze the man's eyes widened and his mouth opened as if to speak, but Meg got there first.

"Oh no, you've scraped yourself," Meg directed her words to the child, smiling gently and completely ignoring the father, "why don't we go inside where we can get you cleaned up? And we can get Billy sorted too, I promise, I'll get him as good as new. And there's biscuits," she added for good measure. She was acting on impulse and Meg really had no idea why she'd invited them in, other than she felt a responsibility for the child's injuries. Under any other circumstances, she would have turned her back on the odious bloke and left him to his own apparent dissatisfaction with the world.

"There's really no need, I'll…" the man began quickly, only to be quietened by his daughter who squirmed to be put down.

"Thank you, Billy would like that," she nodded decisively like a tiny grown up, her blonde curls bobbing as Meg lifted the bucket and picked up the soggy bear that had borne the brunt of the watery episode.

Apparently where the daughter went, the man thankfully followed without further objection, only a large sigh escaping him as he trailed after the pair into the cool darkness of the shop.

When the blood had been gently wiped away, with the girl sitting on her dad's knee and Meg dabbing with a damp, clean cotton wool pad of the sort she normally used for make-up removal, it revealed only a small amount of tiny scratches. The little one milked the event for all it was worth, of course, needing a glass of apple juice and two chocolate digestives in order to sit through the whole ordeal and then a bourbon cream to endure the application of a plaster to each of the injured knees. Meg smiled as she finished the task, and tried to shove her long, unruly hair back under the old headscarf she had put on in haste that morning. If she hadn't already found the man to be incredibly disagreeable she might even have considered the small uptick in the side of his face as his stroked his daughter's hair an actual supressed smile. As it was, the expression was so fleeting Meg couldn't be sure she had even seen it.

Small town and small child aside, Meg was not in the habit of inviting strangers into her space however safe the situation may appear to be and so had left the shop door wide open and declined from inviting the pair up to her home in the flat above. The father and daughter duo were therefore perched on the sole wooden chair in the space, the latter on her dad's lap, surrounded by boxes and bubble wrap which to be honest Meg hadn't had the heart to begin unpacking. The antique chair itself had been left by the shop's previous owners, and Meg wasn't convinced it could support the weight of the huge stranger for very long. Nevertheless, she had tended the child slowly and gently, distracting her by making silly faces and jokes. The man had remained stoic, other than that one, blink-and-you'll-miss-it slip towards the end.

"Now Billy!" The girl shouted, jumping from her father's knee happily as if the whole incident had not occurred and spraying biscuit crumbs onto Meg's head, where she still knelt by the chair. It was an uncomfortable position, to be sure, especially as Meg was determined not to catch the man's eye every time she looked up at his daughter. More than once she had felt his harsh stare boring into her as she worked and had been tempted to match him, glare for glare, but had refrained in the interests of getting this over with as civilly as possible and the rude stranger out of her space. He hadn't even introduced himself for goodness sakes! Talk about bad manners.

"Now Betsie, we can deal with Billy Bear ourselves at home, we need to be getting back now, I've work to do," the bloke said, bending down to retrieve the sodden animal who was still balanced on and dripping into the now upright bucket.

"No!" The girl began to cry again, "I want Aunt Jenna, I want Aunt Jenna…"

"Jenna is still tidying up at Little Acorns," the man said softly – with his daughter, at least, Meg noted, he seemed to have unlimited amounts of patience, "you'll see her at nursery again tomorrow morning."

If it surprised her that the girl cried for an aunt and not her mother, Meg didn't let it show in her expression, simply crouching down beside the child once again. The tear-stained face, the tightly balled, tiny fists and the wild curls that had long since come loose from her ponytail tugged at a place deep in Meg's chest. The place that had always held the hope that this new beginning would finally persuade Chris it was time to start a family.

Feeling her own tears threatening, and having to talk around the lump in her throat, Meg spoke calmly and softly, "Betsie, you really do have to do what Daddy tells you, but if you would like to leave Billy here with me then I can have him washed and dried back to his old self by tomorrow."

"Only one night," the girl said morosely.

"Yes, I'll just have him for one…"

"What she means," the guy barked, "is that she only has the bear for one night, then it will be passed on to tomorrow's Star of the Day at preschool to take home."

"Oh! Well, if I put him in the washing machine now he'll dry quickly out in the back yard in this weather and then I could drop him off to you," again Meg spoke placatingly directly to the girl, ignoring the father who waited impatiently in the doorway.

"Yes please," Betsie replied, her wet eyelashes shimmering with unshed tears.

Her father looked like he was about to object, but clearly thought better of it and, no doubt seeing this as the only way he was going to persuade his daughter to leave – especially since she was now eying up the packet of chocolate digestives once again – he nodded brusquely, "Very well, we live in Upper Oakley, though, above Pinewood Pictures, do you have a vehicle? It's a long walk up the hill otherwise. We're next to the Royal Oak Inn on Castle View."

The name of the small art gallery struck a chord in Meg's memory, and she swiftly recalled the rude missive she had been sent two years ago via email in response to a request that the shop stock some of her paintings. Noting that this man had simply given his address as above the shop, she refused to jump to the assumption that he owned the art studio as well – after all, Meg had already noted that his huge hands would be more suited to other pursuits. Bricklaying and the like. Certainly not fine art. Meg wasn't generally a judgemental person, always trying to see the best in everyone in fact, but this man really had not given her much to work with.

Realising she had tuned out again, Meg forced herself to nod and to the child said, "I'll have him there before bedtime."

Shocked when two chubby arms wrapped themselves around her thighs and squeezed, Meg swallowed down her emotion as the girl was scooped up by her father who stalked out, apparently remembering only in the last moment to say a quick word of thanks.

"Well, I never!" Meg said aloud, in response to the sheer discourteousness of the man. Her heart beat faster in her chest as she watched him stride down the street from the safety of her front step, no doubt reacting to the unfriendly encounter. Nothing to do with the unsettling presence of the man himself.

No, none at all.

Chasing Dreams on Oak Tree Lane

Oak Tree Lane Book One

Publication Date January 15th 2024

Pre-order available now!

A new contemporary, cosy romance series for 2024 set in the beautiful Northumberland countryside, bringing you heartfelt stories and characters you'll fall in love with!

Take a stroll down Oak Tree Lane, the home of cosy community and healing hearts.

Meg always dreamed of moving to Lower Oakley and opening her own art shop. She just never envisaged doing it alone. Faced with the blank canvas that is her new life, she's determined to fill it with colour to match her usually sunny personality.

Josh never dreamed he'd be running his late wife's gallery alone, his little daughter the only light in a life filled with shadows and hurt. Happiest with a hammer and chisel, Josh is hesitant to carve his own path, while his grumpy demeanour is hardly a magnet for a new relationship.

Strange things can happen on Oak Tree Lane, though, when hesitant hearts feel an instant connection.

Can Meg and Josh paper over the cracks of their past losses and paint a new future together?

Or do they not share the same dream after all?

Note from the Author: Whilst some of the residents of Oak Tree Lane will pop up in each book in the series, the stories can be read either in order or as stand alone romances.

ABOUT THE AUTHOR

Rachel Hutchins lives in northeast England with her husband, three children and their dog Boudicca. She loves writing both mysteries and romances, and enjoys reading these genres too! Her favourite place is walking along the local coastline, with a coffee and some cake!

You can connect with via her website at: www.authorrachelhutchins.com

Alternatively, she has social media pages on:

Facebook: www.facebook.com/rahutchinsauthor

Instagram: www.instagram.com/ra_hutchins_author

R. A. Hutchins

OTHER BOOKS BY R. A. HUTCHINS

The Angel and the Wolf

What do a beautiful recluse, a well-trained husky, and a middle-aged biker have in common?
Find out in this poignant story of love and hope!

When Isaac meets the Angel and her Wolf, he's unsure whether he's in Hell or Heaven.
Worse still, he can't remember taking that final step.
They say that calm follows the storm, but will that be the case for Isaac?

Fate has led him to her door,
Will she have the courage to let him in?

To Catch A Feather
Found in Fife Book One

When tragedy strikes an already vulnerable Kate Winters, she retreats into herself, broken and beaten. Existing rather than living, she makes a journey North to try to find herself, or maybe just looking for some sort of closure.

Cameron McAllister has known his own share of grief and love lost. His son, Josh, is now his only priority. In his forties and running a small coffee shop in a tiny Scottish fishing village, Cal knows he is unlikely to find love again.

When the two meet and sparks fly, can they overcome their past losses and move on towards a shared future, or are the memories which haunt them still too real?

These books, as well as others by Rachel, can be found on Amazon worldwide in e-book and paperback formats, as well as free to read on Kindle Unlimited.

Printed in Great Britain
by Amazon